Agatha Christie

Dead Man's Folly

Collins

Collins

HarperCollins Publishers
The News Building
1 London Bridge Street
London SE1 9GF

www.collinselt.com

Collins® is a registered trademark of HarperCollins Publishers Limited.

This *Collins English Readers* edition first published by HarperCollins Publishers 2017.

10 9 8 7 6 5 4 3 2 1

First published in Great Britain by Collins 1956

www.agathachristie.com

ISBN: 978-0-00-824970-0

A catalogue record for this book is available from the British Library.

Cover design © HarperCollins*Publishers* Ltd/Agatha Christie Ltd 2017

Typeset by Davidson Publishing Solutions, Glasgow

Printed and bound by CPI Group (UK) Ltd., Croydon, CR0 4YY

Contents

◆ Introduction ◆

About Collins English Readers

Collins English Readers have been created for readers worldwide whose first language is not English. The stories are carefully graded to ensure that you, the reader, will both enjoy and benefit from your reading experience.

Words which are above the required reading level are underlined the first time they appear in a story. All underlined words are defined in the **Glossary** at the back of the book. Books at levels 1 and 2 take their definitions from the *Collins COBUILD Essential English Dictionary*, and books at levels 3 and above from the *Collins COBUILD Advanced English Dictionary*. Where appropriate, definitions are simplified for level and context.

Alongside the glossary, a **Character list** is provided to help the reader identify who is who, and how they are connected to each other. **Cultural notes** explain historical, cultural and other references. **Maps and diagrams** are provided where appropriate. A **downloadable recording** is also available of the full story. To access the audio, go to www.collinselt.com/eltreadersaudio. The password is the last word on page 4 of this book.

To support both teachers and learners, additional materials are available online at www.collinselt.com/readers. These include a **Plot synopsis** and **classroom activities** (both for teachers), **Student activities**, a **level checker** and much more.

About Agatha Christie

Agatha Christie (1890–1976) is known throughout the world as the Queen of Crime. She is the most widely published and translated author of all time and in any language; only the Bible and Shakespeare have sold more copies.

Agatha Christie's first novel was published in 1920. It featured Hercule Poirot, the Belgian detective who has become the most popular detective in crime fiction since Sherlock Holmes.

Collins has published Agatha Christie since 1926.

The Grading Scheme

The Collins COBUILD Grading Scheme has been created using the most up-to-date language usage information available today. Each level is guided by a comprehensive grammar and vocabulary framework, ensuring that the series will perfectly match readers' abilities.

		CEF band	Pages	Word count	Headwords
Level 1	elementary	A2	64	5,000–8,000	approx. 700
Level 2	pre-intermediate	A2–B1	80	8,000–11,000	approx. 900
Level 3	intermediate	B1	96	11,000–20,000	approx. 1,300
Level 4	upper-intermediate	B2	112-128	15,000–26,000	approx. 1,700
Level 5	upper-intermediate+	B2+	128+	22,000–30,000	approx. 2,200
Level 6	advanced	C1	144+	28,000+	2,500+
Level 7	advanced+	C2	160+	*varied*	*varied*

For more information on the Collins COBUILD Grading Scheme go to www.collinselt.com/readers/gradingscheme.

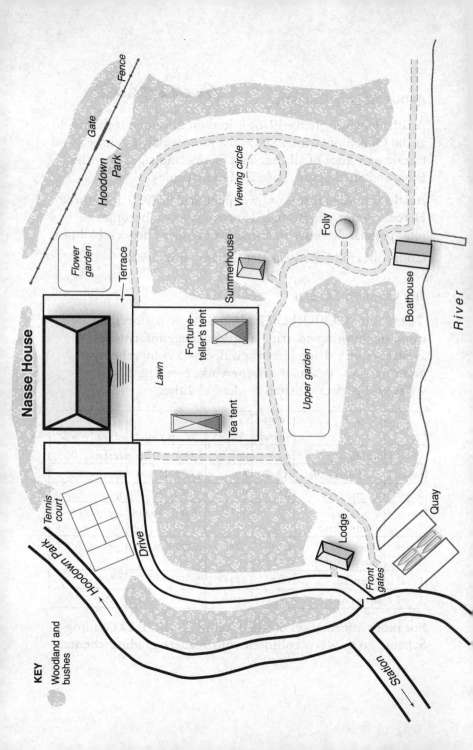

CHAPTER 1

It was Miss Lemon, Poirot's secretary, who picked up the telephone.

'It's Mrs Ariadne Oliver,' she told Poirot.

A memory came into Poirot's mind of a lady with untidy grey hair, and a sharp face.

He took the telephone.

'This is Hercule Poirot,' he announced.

'Monsieur Poirot,' said Mrs Oliver in her magnificent voice. 'I don't know if you'll remember me…'

'Oh, of course I remember you, Madame. Who could forget you?'

'Well, people do,' said Mrs Oliver. 'Perhaps it's because I'm always changing my hair. Look, I *need* you. Immediately. Come by the twelve o'clock train from London. You've got forty-five minutes if my watch is right – though it isn't usually.'

'But where are you, Madame? What is all this about?'

'Nasse House, Nassecombe, Devon[1]. A car will meet you at the station.'

'But what is this *about*?' Poirot repeated.

'Telephones are in such difficult places[2],' said Mrs Oliver. 'This one's in the hall… People passing and talking… I can't really hear. But I'll be waiting for you. Everybody will be *so* excited to see you. Goodbye.'

She put down the phone.

'Ariadne Oliver, writer of detective novels,' said Poirot to Miss Lemon, 'wants me to go to Devon – immediately.'

Miss Lemon looked surprised and not very pleased.

'For what reason?'

'She did not tell me.'

'How very strange. Why not?'

'Because,' said Hercule Poirot, thinking hard, 'she was afraid that someone would hear her.'

'These artists and writers are a bit mad,' said Miss Lemon. 'They're not very sensible at all. How can she think you'd hurry down to Devon for no reason—?'

Poirot waved his hand. 'Please call me a taxi immediately.'

At Nassecombe station, only Hercule Poirot left the train. A large car was parked outside and a driver came forward.

'Mr Hercule Poirot?' he asked with respect.

They drove away from the station along a country lane between high <u>bushes</u>. After a while, they had a beautiful view of a river with hills behind. The driver turned the car a little way off the road and stopped.

'What a magnificent view!' said Poirot. Two girls passed, climbing slowly up the hill. They were carrying heavy <u>rucksacks</u> and wore shorts, with bright scarves over their heads.

'There's a youth hostel[3] next door to us, sir,' explained the driver, who had clearly made himself Poirot's guide to Devon. 'Hoodown Park. It's completely full in summer time, over a hundred people a night.'

Poirot <u>nodded</u>. 'Those girls' rucksacks look heavy,' he said quietly.

'Yes, sir, and it's two miles to Hoodown Park,' said the driver. He paused. 'If you don't mind, sir, could we give them a lift?'

'Certainly,' said Poirot. He was in an almost empty car and here were two young women carrying heavy rucksacks. The driver drove up beside the girls. They looked up in a hopeful way.

Poirot opened the door and they got into the car.

'It is kind of you, thank you,' said one of the girls. She had fair hair and a strong accent.

The other girl, who had a face that was brown from the sun and golden-brown hair showing under her <u>headscarf</u>, nodded, smiled and said, '*Grazie* – Thank you.'

The fair girl continued in a cheerful voice.

'I came to England from Holland for a two-week holiday. I like England. I see Exeter and Torquay – very nice – and tomorrow I cross river to Plymouth[1].'

'And you, Mademoiselle?' Poirot asked. But the other girl just smiled and <u>shook</u> her head.

'She does not speak much English,' said the Dutch girl. 'We both speak a little French – so we talked in French on the train. She is from Italy.'

The driver stopped at a place where the road divided into two parts. The girls got out, said thank you in two languages, and took the left-hand road. The driver turned right into thick woods.

'There are nice young women at that hostel,' he said, 'but they're always <u>trespassing</u>, coming through our woods, and <u>pretending</u> they don't understand it's *not allowed*.' He shook his head.

They soon went through big iron gates, and along a <u>drive</u> to a large white house looking out over the river.

A tall, black-haired <u>butler</u> appeared on the steps.

'Mrs Oliver is expecting you, sir. She went for a walk in the woods.'

He showed Poirot a path through the wood with views of the river below. The path went down until it arrived at last at a viewing circle, a round open space with a low wall.

Mrs Oliver, who was sitting on the wall, stood up. As she got up, she dropped some apples on the ground.

'I don't know why I always drop things,' she said, with her mouth full of apple. 'How are you, Monsieur Poirot?'

'Very well, my dear Madame. And you?'

Mrs Oliver had again, as she had said, changed her hair. It was not the same hairstyle as Poirot remembered. Today, her hair was very curly. She was wearing a wool coat and skirt.

'I knew you'd come,' she said in a cheerful voice.

'You could not know,' said Poirot. 'I still ask myself *why* I am here.'

'Well, I know the answer. You're curious.'

There was a smile in Poirot's eyes. 'You have the famous ability of women to guess correctly.'

He looked round.

'It is a beautiful place.'

'It belongs to some people called Stubbs.'

'Who are they?'

'Oh, nobody really,' said Mrs Oliver. 'Just rich. I've been employed to arrange a murder.'

Poirot looked at her in surprise.

'Not a real one,' said Mrs Oliver. 'There's a <u>fête</u> tomorrow and they wanted to do something new, so there's going to be a Murder Hunt. Like a <u>treasure hunt</u>. They offered me a big fee to plan it.'

'How does it work?'

'You pay to enter and you get shown the first <u>clue.</u> You've got to find the <u>victim</u>, and the <u>weapon</u> and say who did it and what the <u>motive</u> was. And there are prizes.'

'Wonderful!' said Poirot.

'Actually,' said Mrs Oliver, 'it's much harder to arrange than you'd think. Because there's the possibility that real people are going to be intelligent – and in my books I don't have to worry about that.'

'And is that why you have sent for me?' asked Poirot.

'Oh *no*,' said Mrs Oliver. 'Of course not.'

She pulled her ear, thinking.

'Perhaps I'm a fool,' she said. 'But I think there's something wrong.'

CHAPTER 2

'*Wrong*? How?' Poirot asked quickly.

'I don't know... That's what I want *you* to find out. But I've felt, more and more, that someone was... *making me go in the direction they want me to go...* I can only say that if there is a *real* murder tomorrow instead of a false one, I will not be surprised!'

She looked at Poirot.

'I suppose you think I'm a fool,' she said.

'I have never thought of you as a fool,' said Poirot. 'I believe you have noticed things – small things – and they have made you anxious.'

'But it makes me feel so silly,' said Mrs Oliver, 'not to be able to be *sure*.'

'Explain more clearly what you mean by *making you go in the direction they want*,' Poirot said.

'Well... You see, this is *my* murder. I've planned it very carefully and it all fits. And if you know anything about writers, you'll know that they don't like suggestions from other people. People say "That's great, but wouldn't it be better if the murderer were A instead of B?" I mean, I want to say: "Write it yourself if you want it that way!"'

Poirot nodded.

'And has this been happening?'

'Not really... That sort of silly suggestion has been made, and then I've become angry, and the person hasn't said anything more about it. But then they have just quietly made some other suggestion about something not very important at all – and because I've refused to accept the first thing, I've accepted the second without noticing much.'

'Yes,' said Poirot. 'It is a method; something silly is suggested, but that is not the aim. The second, smaller change is really the aim.'

'That's exactly what I mean,' said Mrs Oliver. 'And it's made me worried.'

'Who has made these suggestions?'

'Different people,' said Mrs Oliver. 'Although I think it is really one person working through other people – people who don't know that anything is going on.'

'Do you have any idea who that person is?'

Mrs Oliver shook her head.

'It's somebody very clever and careful,' she said.

'Who is there?' asked Poirot. 'There cannot be many people here?'

'Well, Sir George Stubbs[4] owns this place,' began Mrs Oliver. 'He's rich and very stupid in most ways, I think, but probably very smart about business.

'And there's Lady Stubbs[4] – Hattie – who's about twenty years younger than he is, beautiful, but very stupid too – in fact, *I* think she's a complete fool. She married him for his money, of course, and doesn't think about anything but clothes and jewellery.

'Then there's Michael Weyman – he's an architect, quite young, and good-looking. He's designing a tennis pavilion for Sir George and repairing the folly[5].'

'Folly? What is that?'

'One of those small white buildings that rich people like to have in their gardens. Then there's Miss Brewis, Sir George's secretary – not attractive at all but very efficient. And there are people who come in and help. Young Sally Legge who rents a cottage down by the river with her husband. He's a scientist – very clever but busy with work all the time. Sally's a lovely girl, she's an artist and often comes to the house to help.

'There's Mrs Masterton. She's the wife of the local Member of Parliament[6], very good at organizing.

'Then there's Jim Warburton. He's the Mastertons' political agent[6]. And old Mrs Folliat who lives in the Lodge[7]. Her husband's family were the first owners of Nasse. But when her husband and sons died there were lots of death duties[8] to pay so she sold the place.'

Poirot returned to the main subject.

'Whose idea was the Murder Hunt?'

'Mrs Masterton's, I think.'

'And what explanation did you give about why I am here?' Poirot asked.

'That was easy,' said Mrs Oliver. 'You're here to give out the prizes for it. Everybody's excited. I said I knew you and could persuade you to come.'

Mrs Oliver glanced at her watch.

'It's teatime. Let's go back to the house and you can meet everybody.'

She took a different path from the one by which Poirot had come.

'We pass the <u>boathouse</u> this way,' Mrs Oliver explained.

As she spoke, Poirot saw the boathouse. It was a pretty building by the edge of the river.

'That's where the body for the Murder Hunt is going to be,' said Mrs Oliver.

'I see. And who is going to be killed?'

'Oh, a traveller with a rucksack. But she's really the Yugoslavian first wife of a young <u>atomic scientist</u>,' said Mrs Oliver quickly.

Poirot looked surprised.

'Of course, at first it looks like the atomic scientist killed her – but it's not as simple as that.'

'Of course not – since *you* are involved.'

Mrs Oliver waved her hand.

'Actually,' she said, 'she's killed by the country <u>squire</u> – and the motive is really rather clever – I don't believe many people will understand it, though it's completely clear in the fifth clue.'

Poirot asked an important question:

'How do you arrange for a suitable body?'

'A Girl Guide[9],' said Mrs Oliver. 'Sally Legge was going to be the body, but now they want her to do the <u>fortune-telling</u>. So it's a local Girl Guide called Marlene Tucker. When she hears someone coming, she has to lie down on the floor with a <u>cord</u> round her neck. It's going to be rather boring for the poor girl, staying inside that boathouse until she's found. But I've got some magazines for her – and I've written a clue for the hunt on one of them. We go up this way now.'

They began walking up a steep path that took them back towards the house. Turning between the trees they came into a space with a small white building. A young man, wearing very old trousers and a horrible green shirt, was <u>frowning</u> at it. He turned towards them.

'Mr Michael Weyman, Monsieur Hercule Poirot,' said Mrs Oliver.

'Ah, the architect,' thought Poirot, smiling to himself at Michael Weyman's choice of clothes.

'It's extraordinary,' the young man said angrily, 'the places where people *put* things! This folly, for instance. It was built about a year ago – it's rather nice and fits with the period when the house was built. But why did they put it *here*? These things were meant to be *seen*. It should be in a high, open place with grass all around. But here's this poor little folly, hidden away among trees.'

'Perhaps there wasn't any other place,' said Mrs Oliver.

Michael Weyman made an angry sound.

'The upper garden in front of the house – that's the perfect place. But no, these rich businessmen are all the same – they have no idea about art. Sir George built it here because a tree had fallen in a storm so it seemed like a "good opportunity" to build something. Really, a man like that shouldn't be allowed to own a place like this!'

'This young man certainly does not like Sir George Stubbs,' Poirot thought to himself.

'The floor of the folly is made of <u>concrete</u>,' said Weyman. 'But it's damaged and will become dangerous soon. It would be better to take away the whole thing. That's my advice, but the stupid old fool won't listen to me.'

'What about the tennis pavilion?' asked Mrs Oliver.

The young man looked even more depressed. 'Sir George wants me to design a tower,' he said in an unhappy voice. 'Who would want to be an architect? People who want something good haven't got the money to pay for it, and people who have the money want something awful!'

'I can understand how you feel,' said Poirot in a kind voice.

'George Stubbs,' said the architect. 'Who does he think he is? He had a safe Admiralty job[10] on land in Wales during the war[11] – and then he grew a beard to suggest he was with the <u>Navy</u> at sea. Well, he wasn't! And he has too much money – absolutely too much!'

'Well, architects need people with money, or you'd never have a job,' Mrs Oliver said.

All three began walking towards the house.

The path came out from the trees and the house appeared, white and beautiful with dark trees around it.

Below them a small elderly lady was busy cutting the dead wood from some bushes with a large pair of garden scissors. She climbed up to greet them, breathing a little fast.

'Nothing has been properly looked after for years,' she said. 'And it's so difficult now to find someone who understands plants. This hill would be alive with colour if all this dead wood had been cut out last autumn.'

'Monsieur Hercule Poirot, Mrs Folliat,' said Mrs Oliver.

The elderly lady smiled happily.

'So this is the great Monsieur Poirot! It *is* kind of you to help us tomorrow. This clever lady has thought of an idea for a wonderful Murder Hunt.'

Poirot was confused. She was behaving in every way, like she still owned the place.

He said politely: 'Mrs Oliver is an old friend. I was delighted to come. This is a beautiful place, and what a marvellous house.'

Mrs Folliat nodded.

'Our family has lived here since 1598. The previous house burned down. This one was built by my husband's family in 1790.'

Her voice showed no feeling. Poirot looked at her more carefully. He saw a very small person, dressed in old clothes. Her hair was grey but her eyes were a clear blue. Although she did not care about her appearance, she had that strange quality of *being someone*.

As they walked towards the house, Poirot said, 'It must be hard for you to have strangers living here.'

There was a strange lack of feeling in Mrs Folliat's answer.

'So many things are hard, Monsieur Poirot.'

CHAPTER 3

Mrs Folliat led them into the house, through a small sitting room and into a big <u>drawing room</u>. It was full of people who all seemed to be talking at once.

'George,' said Mrs Folliat, 'this is Monsieur Poirot.'

Sir George, who had been talking in a loud voice, turned round. He was a big man with a red face and a beard. It made him look like an actor who had not decided what part he was playing. It certainly did not make Poirot think of the Navy, in spite of what Michael Weyman had said. His behaviour and voice were cheerful, but his pale blue eyes were small and clever.

He greeted Poirot in a friendly way.

'We're so glad Mrs Oliver persuaded you to come,' he said.

He looked round. 'Hattie!'

Lady Stubbs was lying in a big armchair, smiling down at her hand. She was turning it from left to right, so that a huge <u>emerald</u> on her third finger caught the light.

She looked up like a <u>startled</u> child when her husband approached with Poirot, then politely said, 'How do you do?'

Poirot <u>bowed</u> over her hand.

Sir George continued introducing people to Poirot. 'Mrs Masterton.'

Mrs Masterton was a big woman with eyes that were a little red. She bowed and went on talking.

'This silly problem about the tea tent has got to be solved, Jim,' she said in a loud, strong voice. 'We can't have these local women's stupid arguments.' Both her appearance and her voice made Poirot think of a large kind of dog.

'Right,' said the man she was talking to.

'This is Jim Warburton,' said Sir George.

Mr Warburton showed a lot of white teeth in a rather thin smile, then continued his discussion with Mrs Masterton, 'Don't worry, I'll solve it. What about the fortune-telling tent? Where shall we put it? By the tree? Or at the far end of the <u>lawn</u> in front of the bushes?'

Sir George continued to introduce people. 'Mrs Legge.'

Sally Legge, an attractive young woman with red hair, nodded in a friendly way, then started a discussion with Mrs Masterton.

'And this,' said Sir George, 'is Miss Brewis, who is in charge of us all.'

Miss Brewis was sitting behind a large silver tea <u>tray</u>. She was a thin, efficient-looking woman of about forty, with a quick, pleasant way of doing things.

'How do you do, Monsieur Poirot. Let me give you some tea.'

'Thank you, Mademoiselle.' He added, 'I see you are all very busy.'

'Yes, indeed. There are always so many things to do at the last minute. I was on the telephone for half the morning.'

She handed Poirot his cup.

'A sandwich, Monsieur Poirot? But perhaps, you would prefer a cream cake?'

Poirot *did* prefer a cream cake, and took one.

Then he went and sat down by Lady Stubbs. She was still letting the light play over the emerald on her hand. She looked up at him with the smile of a happy child.

'Look,' she said. 'It's pretty, isn't it?'

She was wearing a big purple hat and heavy make-up in a style not typical of English women. She had very white skin, bright pink lips and thick dark lines painted around her eyes. Her hair showed under the hat, black and smooth. She was a beautiful woman from a country that was hot and sunny. But it was her eyes that startled Poirot. They had an empty look.

She had asked her question like a child, and Poirot answered her in the way he would talk to a child.

'It is lovely.'

She looked pleased.

'George gave it to me yesterday.' Her voice became very soft. 'He gives me lots of things. He's very kind.'

She watched the green fire shining in the depths of the emerald as her hand moved. Then she said very quietly, 'Do you see? It's trying to tell me something.'

She laughed a loud, mad laugh and Poirot felt a sudden shock.

From across the room Sir George said: 'Hattie.' It was a kind but clear warning.

Lady Stubbs stopped laughing.

Poirot tried to return the conversation to normal:

'Devon is lovely.'

'It's nice during the day,' said Lady Stubbs. 'When it doesn't rain. But there aren't any nightclubs.'

'Ah, you like nightclubs?'

'Oh, *yes*,' said Lady Stubbs. 'There's music and dancing. And I wear my nicest clothes and rings. And all the other women have nice clothes and jewellery, but not as nice as mine.'

She smiled with enormous pleasure.

Poirot felt very sorry for her.

'I like the casino, too.' She moved closer towards him. 'I went to a casino in Monte Carlo once.'

'That must have been very exciting, Madame.'

'Oh, it *was*. George gives me money to play with, but usually I lose it.'

She looked very unhappy.

'That is sad,' Poirot said.

'Oh, it doesn't really matter. George is very rich. It is nice to be rich, don't you think?'

'Very nice,' said Poirot gently. 'Have you been busy preparing for the fête?'

Hattie Stubbs shook her head.

'Oh, no. We employ people to do that.'

'Oh, Hattie.' It was Mrs Folliat who spoke. She had come to sit on the sofa nearby. 'Those are the ideas you grew up with on your island estate. But life isn't like that in England these days. I wish it were.' She sighed. 'Nowadays we have to do nearly everything ourselves.'

Lady Stubbs shrugged.

'I think that's stupid. What's the purpose of being rich if I have to do everything myself?'

'Some people find it fun,' said Mrs Folliat, smiling at her. 'I do. Not all things, but I like working in my garden and preparing for fêtes like this one.'

'Will it be like a party?' asked Lady Stubbs in a hopeful voice.

'Just like a party.'

'With big hats and everyone very stylish?'

'Well, not exactly,' said Mrs Folliat. She added gently, 'But you must try and enjoy country things, Hattie. Why didn't you help us this morning, instead of staying in bed until teatime?'

'I had a headache,' said Hattie, sounding cross. Then her mood changed and she smiled at Mrs Folliat in a kind way.

'But I'll be good tomorrow. I'll do everything you tell me.'

'That's very sweet of you, dear.'

'I've got a new dress to wear. Come upstairs and look.'

Mrs Folliat paused. Lady Stubbs stood up.

'You must come. Please. It's such a lovely dress. Come *now*!'

'Oh, all right.' Mrs Folliat gave a little laugh and got up.

She went out of the room, following Hattie. As she walked away, Poirot was startled to see that a sudden look of complete tiredness had replaced the smile on her face. He wondered to himself if she was ill.

Jim Warburton sat down in the chair Hattie Stubbs had been sitting in.

'Lady Stubbs is a beautiful woman,' he said with a broad smile, watching Sir George going out through a door into the garden with Mrs Masterton and Mrs Oliver. 'George Stubbs is mad about her. Nothing's too good for her! Jewellery, expensive clothes, and a lot of other things as well. I've never discovered whether he realizes she's not very intelligent. He probably thinks it doesn't matter.'

'What nationality is she?' Poirot asked in a curious voice.

'She comes from the West Indies.'

Sally Legge came over to join them.

'Now, Jim,' she said, 'you've got to agree with me. The fortune-telling tent's got to be where we all decided – on the far side of the lawn with the bushes behind it. It's the only possible place.'

'Well, Mrs Masterton doesn't think so.'

'Then you've got to persuade her.'

'Mrs Masterton's my boss.'

'No, her husband is your boss. *He's* the Member of Parliament.'

He gave her his thin smile.

'Yes, that's true, but Mrs Masterton should be the MP. She's the person in charge – as I know very well.'

Sir George came back into the room.

'Oh, there you are, Sally,' he said, moving towards Mrs Legge. 'Where's Amy? She can deal with these local women – she's about the only person who can.'

'She went upstairs with Hattie.'

'Oh, did she?'

Sir George looked round and Miss Brewis jumped up. 'I'll fetch her, Sir George.'

'Thank you, Amanda. We must get some more <u>fences</u>,' Sir George continued, 'for where our <u>grounds</u> join Hoodown Park. That's where they get through.'

'Who get through?' Sally Legge asked.

'<u>Trespassers</u>!' cried Sir George. 'They've been a problem since the youth hostel opened. They come from everywhere. They can't speak English properly and they don't understand what you're saying. All kinds of nationalities. And the girls laugh in a silly way.'

'Oh, George, don't start talking about the students,' said Mrs Legge. 'I'll help you deal with them.' She led him out of the door.

CHAPTER 4

'Monsieur Poirot, come and see the clues for the Murder Hunt with us.'

Mrs Oliver and Jim Warburton had come in together from the garden.

Poirot followed them across the hall and into an office.

'The weapons are on your left,' said Warburton. On a small table were a gun, a metal pipe, a bottle with the word _Poison_ on the label and a long thin cord.

'And here are the <u>suspects</u>,' said Mrs Oliver.

She handed Poirot a printed card, which he read with interest.

> Suspects:
>
> Estelle Glynne – a beautiful young woman, guest of…
> Squire Richard Blunt – whose daughter is married to…
> Peter Gaye – a young atomic scientist
> Miss Willing – a secretary
> Quiett – a butler
> Maya Stavisky – a girl traveller
> Esteban Loyola – an unexpected guest

'What an interesting group of people,' Poirot said politely, wondering if Mrs Oliver took her characters from real life. 'But, Madame, what does the competitor do?'

'Turn the card over,' said Jim Warburton.

On the other side was printed:

Name and address:
Name of murderer:
Weapon:
Motive:
Time and place:
Reasons for your conclusions:

'Everyone gets one of these,' explained Warburton. 'There will be six clues. You move from one to the other like in a treasure hunt, and the weapons are hidden. Here's the first clue – a photo. Everyone starts with one of these too.'

Poirot looked at it carefully, frowning. Then he turned it round, looking confused. Warburton laughed.

'Clever, isn't it?' he said. 'It's simple when you know what it is.'

Poirot, who did not know what it was, felt annoyed.

'Is it some kind of window?' he suggested.

'No, it's a section of a tennis net.'

'Ah.' Poirot looked at the photo again. 'Yes, as you say, it is quite obvious when you have been told what it is!'

'So much depends on *how* you look at a thing,' laughed Warburton.

'That is very true.'

'The second clue will be in a box under the tennis net. In the box is this empty bottle of poison.'

'And of course, there's a story,' said Mrs Oliver. She turned to Jim Warburton. 'Have you got the leaflets with the story?'

'They haven't arrived from the printers yet.'

'But they *promised*!'

'Don't worry, they'll be ready at six. I'm going to fetch them.'

'Oh, good.'

Mrs Oliver sighed and turned to Poirot. 'Well, I'll have to *tell* you, then. Only I'm not very good at telling things. I know how to write things clearly, but if I talk it always sounds confused; that's why I never discuss what's going to happen in my stories with anyone.'

Mrs Oliver paused for breath, then said: 'Well, it's like this. There's Peter Gaye who's a young atomic scientist, and he's married to this girl, Joan Blunt, and his first wife Maya is dead, but she isn't really, and she suddenly arrives because she's a secret agent, or perhaps not, I mean she may really just *be* a traveller. Anyway, the wife's in love with another man, and this man Loyola arrives either to meet Maya, or to spy on her, and there's a letter which might be from the secretary, or the butler, and the gun is missing, and you don't know who the letter's to…'

Mrs Oliver stopped, correctly guessing what Poirot was thinking.

'I know,' she said. 'The story sounds very confused, but it isn't – not in my head – and when you see it written down, you'll find it's clear.'

Poirot did not feel sure about that at all.

'Well,' said Jim Warburton, 'I'd better go to the printers.'

He left and Mrs Oliver immediately took Poirot's arm and demanded:

'Have you found anything?'

'Everything seems normal,' Poirot replied. 'Or rather, perhaps that is not quite true. Lady Stubbs is definitely not normal—'

'Shh!' said Mrs Oliver before Poirot had really begun. 'Someone's coming.'

Miss Brewis appeared at the door.

'There you are, Monsieur Poirot. Let me take you to your room.'

She led him upstairs to a big room looking out over the river.

Poirot looked round happily at the bookcase, the reading lamp and the box with the label 'Biscuits' by the bed.

'You have organized everything beautifully. Should I thank you, or Lady Stubbs?'

'Lady Stubbs spends all her time being charming,' said Miss Brewis in a cold voice.

'A very attractive young woman,' said Poirot. 'But in other ways, perhaps a little…' He stopped. 'I'm sorry. I should not say these things.'

Miss Brewis gave him a calm look. 'Lady Stubbs knows exactly what she's doing. She's a very attractive young woman, and she is also a very smart one.'

She had left the room before Poirot had recovered from his surprise.

From the window he saw Lady Stubbs come out of the house with Mrs Folliat, who, carrying her basket, went off down the drive. Lady Stubbs walked down a path that went through the trees to the river.

'Is Madame Oliver right? *Is* there something wrong here?' Poirot asked himself. 'I think there is. But what? I need to know much more about the people in this house.' He thought for a moment, then hurried downstairs.

Poirot walked as fast as he could and managed, breathing quickly, to reach Mrs Folliat and her basket.

'Madame, may I carry this home for you?'

'Oh, thank you, Monsieur Poirot, that's very kind. It's not far. I live in the Lodge by the front gate.'

The Lodge of her former home... How did she really feel about *that*, Poirot wondered. He said:

'Lady Stubbs is much younger than her husband, is she not?'

'Yes, twenty-three years younger.'

'She is very attractive.'

Mrs Folliat said quietly:

'Hattie is a good child.'

It was not an answer he had expected. Mrs Folliat continued:

'I know her very well, you see. I looked after her for a while. It's a sad story. Her family had a large sugar business in the West Indies. Then the house burned down in an accident and her family died. Hattie was at school in Paris and so was suddenly left without any close relatives. I became in charge of her.' Mrs Folliat added with a dry smile: 'I knew the right people to ask – the top man in the West Indies had been a close friend of ours.'

'Of course, Madame, I understand.'

'It was very convenient for me – I was going through a difficult time. My husband had died before the war and my older son, who was in the Navy, died too when his ship sank. My younger son, who had been out in Kenya, came back, joined the Army and was killed in Italy. That all meant death duties and this house had to be sold to pay them. I went over to Paris to meet Hattie and that's where we got to know each other. We lived there very happily as mother and daughter until she married. I was glad to have someone young to look after. I became very fond of Hattie – especially, perhaps, because she didn't have the ability to look after herself. Hattie is not very clever, Monsieur Poirot. It's very easy to <u>influence</u> her. It was good that she had no money. If she had been rich, things would have been much more difficult. She was attractive to men and, being very friendly, was easily controlled – she definitely needed to be looked after. So I could only be grateful when Sir George Stubbs wanted to marry her.'

'Yes, it was a solution.'

'Sir George is a successful businessman,' said Mrs Folliat, 'but he's kind as well as very rich. Hattie is everything he wants. She displays clothes and jewellery beautifully, loves him and wants to please him, and is completely happy with him. I'm very grateful about that, because I admit I persuaded her to accept him. If the marriage had not been a success…' Her voice shook.

'It seems to me,' said Poirot, 'that you made a very sensible arrangement for her.' He added: 'As for Nasse House, it is just beautiful.'

'Since Nasse had to be sold,' said Mrs Folliat, 'I'm glad that it was Sir George who bought it.'

They were now standing by the front gate. The Lodge, a small white building, was situated a little way back from the drive.

Mrs Folliat took her basket from Poirot and thanked him.

'I was always fond of the Lodge,' she said, looking at it with love. 'Merdell, our head gardener for thirty years, used to live here.' She sighed. 'There's hardly anybody left now on the estate from the old days – it's all new faces.'

'I am glad, Madame, that you have found somewhere safe and quiet to be happy.'

She paused and said without any change in her voice: 'It's a very wicked world, Monsieur Poirot. And there are very wicked people in it. You probably know that as well as I do… Yes, it's a very wicked world…'

She smiled at him and went into the Lodge.

CHAPTER 5

Poirot felt like exploring so instead of returning immediately to the main house, he went through the front gates and down the steep road that came out onto a small <u>quay</u>. There was a large bell with a notice saying *Ring for the Ferry*. There were several boats tied up to the quay. A very old man with weak red eyes moved slowly towards Poirot.

'Do you want the ferry, sir?'

'No, thank you. I have just come down from Nasse House for a walk.'

'Ah, I worked there as a boy, I did – and my son, he was head gardener there. But I looked after the boats. Old Squire Folliat went out sailing in every kind of weather. His son didn't like sailing. He only cared about horses. He spent a lot of money on them. He spent a lot of money on drinking too – his wife had a hard time with him. You've maybe seen her – she lives at the Lodge now.'

'Yes, I have just left her there now.'

'She's a Folliat, too. She loves the garden and all those flowers and bushes. Even when the Army were staying in the house and her two sons had gone to the war, she still took care of that garden.'

'It was hard for her, both her sons being killed.'

'Ah, she's had a hard life. She had trouble with her husband and her son. Not her older son, Mr Henry. He was as nice as you could wish, but the younger son, Mr James, gave her a lot of trouble. He owed people money, he liked women, and he got angry very quickly.'

'So now,' said Poirot, 'there are no more Folliats at Nasse.'

The old man suddenly stopped talking.

'Just as you say, sir.'

Poirot looked at the old man in a curious way.

'Instead you have Sir George Stubbs. What do local people think about him?'

'We're told,' said the old man, 'that he's very rich.'

'And his wife?'

'Ah, she's not interested in gardens. They say she's not very intelligent.'

The old man paused, then continued.

'But she's always very polite and friendly. They've been here just over a year. I remember the day they arrived. It was in the evening, after the worst storm I ever remember. The wind blew trees down everywhere – one was blown down across the drive and we had to move it in a hurry to get the drive clear for their car. And there was another big tree down in the woods too – that one brought a lot of others down with it, which made a terrible mess.'

'Ah, yes, is that where the folly is now?'

'Mmmm,' the old man said, frowning. 'It's called a folly and it is a folly[4]. There never was a folly in the old Folliats' time. That thing was Lady Stubbs' idea. It was built less than three weeks after they came. It looks so silly there among the trees.'

Poirot smiled. 'These ladies have their own ideas,' he said. 'It is sad that the time of the Folliats is over.'

'Oh, don't believe that, sir.' The old man laughed. 'There will always be Folliats at Nasse.'

'But the house belongs to Sir George Stubbs.'

'Perhaps it does – but there's still a Folliat here. Ah! The Folliats are very smart!'

'What do you mean?'

The old man glanced at him, paused, then said:

'Well, Mrs Folliat is living in the Lodge, isn't she?' Then he walked slowly away.

◆ ◆ ◆

At dinner that evening, there were candles on the long table and the room was full of shadows.

Sally Legge and Jim Warburton had both stayed for dinner.

'We have a busy evening ahead of us,' Jim Warburton warned. 'There are notices to make, and the big sign for the fortune-telling. What name shall we have? Madame Zuleika?'

'Yes, Zuleika sounds all right,' said Sally.

There was some general conversation about preparing things for the next day but Lady Stubbs didn't say anything. As they came out of the room after dinner, she stopped by the stairs.

'I'm going to bed,' she announced. 'I'm very sleepy.'

'Oh, Lady Stubbs,' cried Miss Brewis, 'there's so much to do.'

'Yes, I know,' said Lady Stubbs. 'But I'm going to bed.' She spoke happily, like a small child.

Sir George touched her shoulder.

'You go and sleep, Hattie. Be fresh for tomorrow.'

He kissed her and she went up the stairs, calling out:

'Goodnight, everybody.'

Sir George smiled up at her.

Miss Brewis made an annoyed sound and turned quickly away.

'Come along, everybody,' she said, trying to speak in a cheerful voice. 'We've got work to do.'

◆ ◆ ◆

Poirot came down to breakfast the following morning at nine-thirty. Sir George was eating a huge breakfast of eggs and bacon. Mrs Oliver and Miss Brewis were having the same, but in smaller amounts.

Lady Stubbs was biting into some toast and drinking black coffee. She was wearing a large pale-pink hat, which looked strange at the breakfast table.

Miss Brewis was quickly looking through the post. She passed Sir George any letters that had *Personal* written on them. The others she opened herself.

Lady Stubbs had three letters. She opened what were clearly a couple of bills and threw them to one side. Then she opened the third letter and said suddenly and clearly:

'Oh!'

She sounded so startled that everybody looked at her.

'It's from Etienne,' she said. 'My cousin. He's coming here, in his <u>yacht</u>.'

'Let's see, Hattie.' Sir George held out his hand. She passed the letter down the table.

'Who's this Etienne de Sousa? A cousin, you say?'

'I don't remember him well. He was...'

'Yes?'

She shrugged.

'It doesn't matter. It was a long time ago. I was a little girl.'

'Well, we must give him a good welcome,' said Sir George. 'It's a pity it's the fête today, but we'll ask him to dinner. Perhaps he could stay with us for a night or two – we could show him something of the country.'

Lady Stubbs looked down into her coffee cup.

Conversation about the fête became general. Only Poirot did not involve himself in it. He was watching Lady Stubbs and wondering what was going on in her mind. At that moment she raised her eyes and glanced quickly along the table to where he sat. It was such an intelligent look that he was startled. As they looked at each other, the look disappeared – her empty eyes returned. But he was sure that other look had been there, cold, watching… Or had he imagined it?

Lady Stubbs got up suddenly.

'I have a headache,' she said. 'I'm going to lie down.'

Sir George jumped up, looking worried. 'Poor girl. You're all right, aren't you?'

'Oh, it's just a headache.'

'You'll be fit for this afternoon?' asked Sir George.

'Yes, probably.'

As she moved towards the door, she dropped the <u>handkerchief</u> she had been holding between her fingers. Poirot, moving quietly, picked it up. Sir George, following his wife, was stopped by Miss Brewis.

'About the car parking this afternoon, Sir George—?'

Poirot reached Lady Stubbs on the stairs.

'Madame, you dropped this.'

He bowed and held out the handkerchief.

She took it without seeming to care very much.

'Thank you.'

'I am very sorry, Madame, that you are not feeling well. Particularly when your cousin is coming.'

She answered quickly, almost angrily.

'I don't want to see Etienne. I don't like him. He was always bad. I'm afraid of him. He does bad things.'

The door opened and Sir George came across the hall and up the stairs.

'Hattie, my poor girl. Let me take you up to bed.'

They went up the stairs together, his arm round her gently, his face worried.

Poirot turned and met Miss Brewis walking quickly and holding papers in her hand.

'Lady Stubbs' headache—' he began.

'Oh, she hasn't got a headache,' said Miss Brewis in an annoyed voice, and disappeared into her office.

Poirot sighed and went out through the front door onto the terrace. Mrs Masterton had just arrived and was organizing people into putting up a large tent for tea.

She turned to greet Poirot.

'Where's Sir George, Monsieur Poirot? I want to talk to him about the tea tent.'

'His wife had a headache and has gone to lie down. He was worried and went upstairs with her. I believe he is still with her.'

'She'll be all right this afternoon,' said Mrs Masterton confidently. 'She likes fêtes, you know. She'll be as pleased about it as a child. Can you give me a hand, please?'

Mrs Masterton made Poirot work hard. She talked to him during his brief periods of rest.

'It's nice that people are living in Nasse again. We were all so afraid it was going to be a hotel. All the houses I stayed in as a girl – or where I went to dances – have become hotels. It's very sad. Yes, I'm glad about Nasse and so is poor Amy Folliat. She's had such a hard life, but she never complains. Sir George has done wonderful things for Nasse. I don't know whether that's because Amy has helped him or because he enjoys things of good quality. He *does* like good quality, you know. It's very surprising in a man like that.'

'Is he not one of the landed gentry[4]?' said Poirot carefully.

'Oh no. He isn't even really *Sir* George. He gave himself the name. It's very amusing, really. Of course, we never tell him we know. Rich men must be allowed to pretend, don't you agree?

The funny thing is that in spite of his ordinary background George Stubbs would actually get on very well anywhere. He acts like a true eighteenth-century country squire.'

Mrs Masterton interrupted herself to shout at a gardener. 'Don't put it by that flower. You must leave room over to the right. *Right* – not left!'

She continued: 'It's extraordinary how they can't tell their left from their right. The Brewis woman is efficient. She doesn't like poor Hattie, though. She looks at her sometimes in a way that makes me think she'd like to murder her. So many of these good secretaries are in love with their bosses. Now where do you think Jim Warburton is? Ah! Sally has come to help.'

Poirot disappeared quietly.

As he came round the corner of the house, he saw something surprising taking place.

Two young women, wearing shorts and bright blouses, had come out from the woods and were standing looking at the house. He recognized the Italian girl they had given a lift to yesterday. Sir George was looking down on the two girls from Lady Stubbs' bedroom window.

'You're trespassing,' he shouted angrily.

'No understand,' said the Italian girl, who was wearing a green headscarf.

'You can't come through here.'

The other young woman, who had a blue headscarf, said in a cheerful voice:

'Nassecombe Quay? Please.'

'You're trespassing,' shouted Sir George.

'Please?'

'*Trespassing!* There's no way through. You've got to go back. *BACK!*'

They talked together in a flood of words in a foreign language. Finally, the girl with the blue headscarf said:

'Back? To hostel?'

'That's right. And use the road – *road* round that way.'

Not looking very happy, they turned and went back. Sir George looked down at Poirot.

'I spend my time telling people to go away,' he said. 'They get over the fences. They think they can get down to the quay this way. Well, they can, of course – it's much quicker. But it's not allowed—

'Yes, Hattie? What did you say?' He disappeared back into the room.

Poirot turned to find Mrs Oliver and a girl of about fourteen dressed in a Girl Guide uniform behind him.

'This is Marlene,' said Mrs Oliver. Marlene laughed.

'I'm the dead body,' she said. 'But I'm not going to have any blood on me.' There was disappointment in her voice.

'No?' asked Poirot.

'No. I just get <u>strangled</u>. I'd *like* to be <u>stabbed</u> – and have lots of red paint.'

'Mr Warburton thought it might look too real,' said Mrs Oliver.

'In a murder I think you should have blood,' said Marlene. She looked at Poirot with interest. 'Have you seen lots of murders? *She* says you have.'

'One or two,' said Poirot.

'Any <u>maniacs</u>?' asked Marlene. 'I like maniacs,' she said happily. 'Reading about them, I mean.'

'You would probably not enjoy meeting one.'

'Oh, I don't know. I believe we've got a maniac round here. My granddad saw a dead body in the woods once. He was scared and ran away, and when he came back it was gone. It was a woman's body. But my granddad's a bit mad too, so no one listens to what he says.'

Poirot managed to escape and hid in his bedroom. He felt in need of a rest.

Chapter 6

At two-thirty a film star (although not a very famous one) opened the fête and by three o'clock everything was very busy. There was a line of cars in the long drive. Students from the youth hostel arrived in groups and, as Mrs Masterton had predicted, Lady Stubbs had come out of her bedroom. She was wearing a dark pink dress with an enormous hat which covered most of her face.

Poirot walked around – everything seemed to be happening as in a normal fête. There were long tables displaying local fruit, vegetables, jams and cakes. There were contests to win cakes and baskets of fruit – visitors could even win a pig.

A display of children's dancing began and Lady Stubbs' pink dress showed clearly among the crowd. The main person of interest, however, seemed to be Mrs Folliat. She had changed completely and was wearing a blue dress and a smart grey hat. She appeared to be in charge of everything, greeting people who had just arrived, and telling people the way to the different attractions.

Poirot stayed near her and listened to some of the conversations.

'Amy, how are you?'

'Oh, Pamela, how nice of you and Edward to come.'

'Dorothy! It's *ages* since I've seen you.'

'We *had* to come and see Nasse looking so marvellous. Amy, you've done wonderful things in the last year. Nasse is really beginning to look like itself again.'

Dorothy's husband said in a loud voice:

'I came over here during the war when the Army was using it. It nearly broke my heart.'

Mrs Folliat turned to greet a more ordinary visitor.

'Mrs Knapper, I'm so pleased to see you. Is this Lucy? How tall she's grown!'

'She'll be leaving school next year. I'm pleased to see you looking so well, Mrs Folliat.'

'I'm very well, thank you. You must go and try some of the activities, Lucy. See you in the tea tent later, Mrs Knapper. I'll be helping with the tea.'

An elderly man – probably Mr Knapper, thought Poirot – said in a rather shy way: 'We're pleased to have you back at Nasse, Mrs Folliat. It seems like the old days.'

Poirot moved slowly away.

He wondered whether Mrs Folliat realized how completely she was behaving like she owned the place. She was, very definitely this afternoon, Mrs Folliat of Nasse House.

Poirot continued walking around the fête. He was standing by a tent with a large sign saying *Madame Zuleika Fortune-Telling* when a woman made him pay some money to guess the weight of a cake.

'Time for the children's <u>fancy dress</u> contest!' called Jim Warburton. 'Make a line, please.'

Poirot moved towards the house and was stopped by the Dutch girl he had met the day before.

'So you have come to the fête,' he said. 'And your friend?'

'Oh, yes, she is coming this afternoon too. I have not seen her yet, but we leave together by the bus that goes from the gates at five-fifteen. We go together to Torquay and there I change to another bus for Plymouth.'

Poirot had been surprised to see that the Dutch girl was carrying a heavy rucksack on her back. Now he understood that it was because she was leaving.

He said: 'I saw your friend this morning.'

'Oh, yes. Elsa, a German girl, was with her. She told me they tried to go through the woods to the river. The man who owns the house was very angry. He made them go back.'

She turned her head to where Sir George was encouraging competitors at one of the games.

'But now he is very polite.'

At that moment Jim Warburton arrived, looking hot and annoyed.

'Have you seen Lady Stubbs, Poirot? She's supposed to be judging the fancy dress contest and I can't find her anywhere.'

'I saw her about half an hour ago.'

'Where can she have disappeared to?' said Warburton angrily. The children are waiting.' He looked round. 'Perhaps she's gone into the house.'

He went away quickly.

Poirot moved through the crowd towards the large tent where tea was being served, but there was a long queue and he decided not to stay.

He went to a place where he could avoid the crowd and watch the activities.

He heard someone approaching him from behind and turned. A young man was coming up the path from the quay; a dark-skinned young man, beautifully dressed in yacht clothes. He paused, a little confused by the fête which he clearly hadn't known was happening.

Then he spoke to Poirot.

'Please excuse me. Is this the house of Sir George Stubbs?'

'It is indeed.' Poirot made a guess. 'Are you, perhaps, the cousin of Lady Stubbs?

'I am, yes – Etienne de Sousa.'

'My name is Hercule Poirot.'

They bowed to each other. Poirot explained what was going on at the fête. As he finished, Sir George came across the lawn.

'De Sousa? I'm delighted to see you. Hattie got your letter this morning. We must find her. She's here somewhere... You'll have dinner with us this evening, I hope?'

'Thank you. You're very kind.'

'Hattie will be delighted, I'm sure,' said Sir George politely. 'Where *is* she? I saw her not long ago.'

He looked round in a confused way.

'She should be judging the children's fancy dress contest. Excuse me a moment. I'll ask Miss Brewis.'

He hurried away.

'Is it some time since you last saw your cousin?' Poirot asked.

De Sousa shrugged his shoulders.

'I haven't seen here since she was fifteen,' he replied. 'She was sent then to school in France. She was still a child, but she was already very good-looking.'

He looked at Poirot.

'She is now a beautiful woman,' said Poirot.

'And that's her husband? He seems a nice man, but perhaps not very smart? Still, for Hattie it was perhaps a little difficult to find a suitable husband.'

Poirot looked at him. 'I'm sorry, I do not understand what you mean,' he said politely.

The other man laughed.

'Oh, it's no secret. At fifteen Hattie's mind was not properly developed. Is she still the same?'

'It seems so, yes,' said Poirot.

De Sousa shrugged.

'Ah, well! Why should we expect women to be intelligent? It isn't necessary.'

Sir George came back, looking very angry. Miss Brewis was with him, speaking rather quickly.

'I've no idea where she is, Sir George. I last saw her over by the fortune-telling tent.'

'Perhaps,' said Poirot, 'she has gone to see Mrs Oliver's Murder Hunt?'

Sir George looked happier.

'That's probably it. Look, I can't leave the fête. I'm in charge. And Amanda's very busy. Could *you* possibly have a look, Poirot?'

Miss Brewis told him approximately where each of the clues were and then led Etienne de Sousa away. Poirot walked off, talking to himself: 'Tennis court, flower garden, upper garden, folly, boathouse…'

As he passed one of the games, he was interested to notice Sir George explaining it with a broad smile of welcome to the same young Italian woman he had sent away that morning. She looked confused – she could not understand the change in his behaviour.

At the tennis court there was only an old man asleep on a garden seat. Poirot went on to the upper garden which was nearby and also very quiet, and then to the flower garden. There he found Mrs Oliver dressed in purple, sitting looking depressed.

'This is only the second clue and nobody's come yet,' she said. 'I think I've made them too difficult. What if *nobody* finds my body?'

'Be patient, Madame,' said Poirot. 'It is still early in the afternoon.'

'That's true,' said Mrs Oliver, looking happier. 'And people can get in for half-price after four-thirty, so lots of people will probably come then. Let's go and see how Marlene is.'

They walked along the path through the woods, passing the folly and going down to the river. They could see the boathouse below them. Poirot asked: 'Is it not possible that the competitors might find the boathouse and the body by accident? That would not be good at all.'

'I thought of that,' replied Mrs Oliver. 'That's why the last clue is a key. You can't open the door without it.'

They followed the path down to the door of the boathouse. Mrs Oliver used her key to open the door.

'We've just come to see how you are, Marlene,' she said in a cheerful voice as she went inside.

Marlene, arranged as 'the body,' was playing her role well, lying on the floor by the window.

She lay without moving.

'It's all right, Marlene,' said Mrs Oliver. 'It's only me and Monsieur Poirot. You can move!'

Poirot was frowning. Very gently he pushed Mrs Oliver to one side and looked closely at the girl on the floor. He said a few words and looked up at Mrs Oliver.

'I am afraid, Madame Oliver...' he said, 'that you were right.'

Mrs Oliver's eyes opened wide. 'You can't mean... She isn't *dead*?'

Poirot nodded. 'Oh, yes. She is dead.'

'But how—?'

He lifted the scarf round the girl's head, so that Mrs Oliver could see the cord.

'Just like *my* murder,' said Mrs Oliver, her voice shaking. 'But *who*? And *why*?'

'That is the question,' said Poirot.

Why had Marlene Tucker, a fourteen-year-old girl from the village without an enemy in the world, become a murder victim?

CHAPTER 7

Inspector Bland[12] sat behind a table in the study at Nasse House. At the boathouse a police photographer was busy taking pictures and the doctor had just arrived.

'What should I do about the fête?' asked Sir George. 'Should I stop it? People are saying that there's been an accident. I don't think anyone's <u>suspected</u> yet that it's murder!'

'Then leave things as they are,' decided Bland. 'How many people are at the fête?'

'A couple of hundred, I think,' answered Sir George, 'and there are more arriving all the time. But I don't see what reason any of them could have to murder a girl like that.'

'She was a local girl, wasn't she?'

'Yes. Her father's a farm worker. Her mother's here at the fête. Miss Brewis – that's my secretary – is giving her cups of tea.'

The Inspector nodded.

'I'll need to speak to both of them. I'll also want to see Lady Stubbs and the people who discovered the body. One of them, I believe, designed this Murder Hunt?'

'That's right. Mrs Ariadne Oliver.'

'Oh!' the Inspector said, 'I've read a lot of her books myself.'

'She's very upset, of course,' said Sir George. 'But I'm afraid I don't know where my wife is. She seems to have disappeared. But she won't be able to tell you much. Who would you like to see first?'

'Your secretary, and after that the girl's mother.'

Sir George nodded and left the room.

Constable Robert Hoskins[12], a local policeman, explained to Bland:

'Lady Stubbs isn't very intelligent. That's why Sir George said she wouldn't be much help.'

Bland nodded. Then he asked a question.

'Who do you think did it, Hoskins?'

If anyone had any ideas about what had been going on, it would be Hoskins, Bland thought. He had a great interest in everybody and everything. He also had a wife who talked a lot – and that, together with his job as local constable, provided him with a huge quantity of information.

'It wouldn't be anyone local. The Tuckers are a nice family. There are nine of them all together, but only the three youngest ones are still living at home.' He paused, thinking. 'None of them are very smart. But Mrs Tucker's home is very clean. The killer will probably be one of those people at the youth hostel at Hoodown. There are some very strange people there.'

The door opened and the doctor walked in.

'This murder was very simple,' he said. 'The girl was strangled with a piece of cord. She probably didn't know what was happening until it had happened.'

'What about the time of death?' Bland asked.

The doctor glanced at his watch.

'It's half past five now. I saw her at twenty past five, and she'd been dead about an hour. I'll let you know if we find out any more information.'

The doctor left the room and Inspector Bland asked Hoskins to bring in Miss Brewis. He felt happier when Miss Brewis came in. Here, he realized at once, was someone who was efficient.

'Mrs Tucker's in my sitting room,' Miss Brewis said as she sat down. 'I've given her some tea. She's very upset, of course. Mr Tucker finishes work at six o'clock and was coming to join his wife here. I've told people to look out for him and to bring him to me when he arrives. The younger children are at the fête and someone is looking after them.'

'Excellent,' said Inspector Bland. 'Before I see Mrs Tucker I'd like to hear what you and Lady Stubbs can tell me.'

'I don't know where Lady Stubbs is,' said Miss Brewis. 'She probably got bored and walked off. What do you want to know?'

'What Marlene Tucker was doing in this Murder Hunt.'

Miss Brewis gave a clear explanation about the Murder Hunt and the plan of the murder story.

'At the beginning, Mrs Legge was going to be the victim,' she continued. 'But then we discovered that Mrs Legge was very good at fortune-telling. So it was decided that she would have a tent for fortune-telling. Then we had to find somebody else to be the dead body. The local Girl Guides were helping at the fête, and someone suggested one of the Guides would be suitable.'

'Who suggested that, Miss Brewis?'

'I'm not sure.'

'Is there any reason why this girl was chosen?'

'I don't think so. Her family rent a cottage on the estate, and her mother sometimes helps in the kitchen. But I don't know why we chose her. Marlene was very pleased to be asked, though. She enjoyed being the body.'

'I noticed a tray in the boathouse with a plate and a glass,' said the Inspector.

'Oh, yes, Lady Stubbs asked me to take Marlene some cakes and a drink.'

Bland looked up, interested.

'What time were you at the boathouse?'

Miss Brewis thought for a moment.

'Let me see. The children's fancy dress contest had been judged. There was a little delay because Lady Stubbs couldn't be found, but Mrs Folliat took her place, so that was all right... Yes, it must have been about quarter past four when I reached the boathouse. I called out and she opened the door. She was very keen to know what was happening in the Murder Hunt.'

She added, 'Was it soon after that...?'

'Yes, it can't have been very long after.'

'Oh, dear,' said Miss Brewis.

'Did you meet anybody or see anyone near the boathouse?'

'No,' Miss Brewis said. 'No one.'

'Is there anything you know about this girl that could help us?' the Inspector asked.

'Nothing,' said Miss Brewis. 'It seems impossible that anyone would murder her.'

Bland sighed.

'I'd better see the mother now.'

Mrs Tucker was a thin woman with blonde hair and a sharp nose. Her eyes were red from crying.

'I'm very, very sorry about this,' said Inspector Bland gently. 'Can you tell me if there is anyone who had any reason to hurt Marlene?'

'I've thought and thought,' said Mrs Tucker. 'But I can't think of anyone. Marlene sometimes had arguments at school, but nothing serious.'

'She never talked about an enemy of any kind?'

'She often talked about silly things, but it was all about make-up and hairstyles. You know what girls are like. She was much too young to wear make-up and we told her that. But whenever she got any money, she'd buy herself perfume and make-up and hide it from us.'

She began to cry.

Still crying, Mrs Tucker was accompanied out of the room by Constable Hoskins.

CHAPTER 8

'I feel awful,' said Mrs Oliver, sitting down in the chair in front of Inspector Bland. 'It's *my* murder. I did it!'

For a startled moment Inspector Bland thought Mrs Oliver was saying that she was the killer.

'I don't know why I wanted the Yugoslavian wife of an atomic scientist to be the victim,' said Mrs Oliver, pushing her hands through her hair.

The Inspector looked at her, trying to decide if he could believe what she said. She was obviously very <u>dramatic</u>.

'I'm not mad,' said Mrs Oliver, guessing what the Inspector was thinking. 'I'm upset. Really upset. Why did anybody murder her?'

'I was hoping,' said the Inspector, 'that you could help me to answer that.'

'I can't help you,' said Mrs Oliver. 'I can't imagine who could have done it. Well, of course, I can *imagine* – I can imagine anything! That's the trouble with me. I can imagine things now – I could even make them sound all right, but of course none of them would be true. For example, perhaps the girl was murdered because she knew that somebody was having a romance, or she saw someone burying a body at night, or she recognized somebody who was trying to hide who he was. Or perhaps the man in the yacht threw somebody into the river and she saw it from the window of the boathouse—'

'Please!' The Inspector held up his hand. He was getting more and more confused

Mrs Oliver stopped. It was clear that she could have continued talking about her ideas for some time, although it seemed to the Inspector she had already thought of every possible explanation. Out of all these ideas he held onto one phrase.

'What did you mean, Mrs Oliver, by "the man in the yacht"?'

'The one we were talking about at breakfast, who came in a yacht,' she said.

'*Please*.' The Inspector knew that Mrs Oliver had written forty books, but it was surprising to him that she had not written a hundred and forty. 'What *is* all this about a man at breakfast who came in a yacht?'

'Oh, he didn't come at breakfast time,' said Mrs Oliver, 'It was a letter to Lady Stubbs that arrived at breakfast time. From a cousin in a yacht. And she was frightened of him and didn't want him to come, and I think that's why she's hiding now.'

'Hiding?' said the Inspector.

'Well, she isn't here,' said Mrs Oliver. 'Everyone's been looking for her. *I* think she's hiding because she doesn't want to meet him.'

'Who *is* this man?' demanded the Inspector.

'You'd better ask Monsieur Poirot,' said Mrs Oliver. 'He spoke to him. His name is Etienne de Sousa.'

But the other name was of great interest to the Inspector.

'Poirot?'

'Yes. Hercule Poirot. He was with me when we found the body.'

'A Belgian, a small man with a very big moustache?'

'An enormous moustache,' agreed Mrs Oliver. 'Yes. Do you know him?'

'Well, I met him many years ago. What's he doing down here?'

Mrs Oliver paused for a moment, then said:

'He was going to give the prizes to the winners of the Murder Hunt.'

'Hmm,' said Bland. 'I'd like to talk to him.'

'Shall I get him for you?' Mrs Oliver asked.

'Yes, thank you very much, madam,' he said.

Mrs Oliver left the room and Constable Hoskins asked with interest:

'Who's this Hercule Poirot, sir?'

'He's a very interesting little Belgian man,' said Inspector Bland. 'But he's also very clever.'

Then Inspector Bland realized that people had told him something several times: nobody could find Lady Stubbs.

'Fetch Lady Stubbs for me,' he said to Constable Hoskins. 'If she isn't here, look for her.'

Hoskins left the room. As he went through the door, he paused to allow Hercule Poirot to enter.

'I don't suppose,' said Bland, getting up and holding out his hand, 'that you remember me, Monsieur Poirot.'

'But of course I do,' said Poirot. 'It is the young sergeant[12] – yes, Sergeant Bland – we met perhaps fifteen years ago.'

'Quite right. What a wonderful memory you have!'

'Not at all. Since you remember me, why should I not remember you?'

It would be difficult to forget Hercule Poirot, Bland thought to himself.

'Mrs Oliver tells me you are here to give the prizes for this Murder Hunt. She didn't stop telling me things. Every possible motive for the girl's murder. She's made me very confused. What an imagination!'

'She earns money from her imagination, my friend,' said Poirot.

'She mentioned a man called de Sousa – did she imagine that?'

'No, he is a fact.'

Poirot told the Inspector about what had happened at the breakfast table, the letter, and Lady Stubbs' headache.

'I'm beginning to have some strange ideas about what's going on here...' said Bland. He stopped as the door opened and Constable Hoskins came in.

'Lady Stubbs is not in the house, sir,' he said. 'Sergeant Farrell and Constable Lorimer are <u>searching</u> the grounds.'

'Find out from the man who's taking money at the gate if she's left the place.'

'Yes, sir.'

Hoskins went out.

'And find out when she was last seen, and where,' Bland shouted after him. He turned back to Poirot. 'Tell me what you know about de Sousa.'

Poirot described his conversation with the young man.

'And when did you last see Lady Stubbs?'

Poirot remembered seeing her huge hat moving around the lawn.

'Not long before four o'clock, near the house.'

'Was she there when de Sousa arrived?'

'No, I did not see her then. Sir George told de Sousa that his wife was somewhere nearby.'

'What time did de Sousa arrive?'

'About half past four.'

'So Lady Stubbs had disappeared before he arrived?'

'Yes, probably.'

'Well, she can't have gone far,' said Bland. 'It should be easy to find her.' He stopped, then changed the subject.

'I just can't understand the murder of Marlene Tucker at all,' he said. 'An ordinary girl is strangled without any motive. Then Mrs Oliver thinks of a dozen motives! Among them was that perhaps Marlene saw somebody being murdered, or something de Sousa did as he was going up the river...

'I think I'd better have a talk with this de Sousa.'

CHAPTER 9

Inspector Bland disliked Etienne de Sousa immediately. The young man was very confident, very relaxed. He also seemed to find everything rather amusing.

'You must admit,' he said, 'that life is full of surprises. I arrive here on my yacht *Espérance*. I admire the beautiful countryside, I come to spend an afternoon with a little cousin that I haven't seen for years – and what happens? First, I find a noisy festival going on all around me, and immediately afterwards, I'm in the middle of a murder.'

He lit a cigarette. 'But this murder doesn't involve me. In fact, I have no idea why you want to interview me.'

'I believe you came up the river this afternoon, Mr de Sousa.'

'That's correct, yes.'

'Did you notice a small boathouse by the edge of the river?'

de Sousa threw back his handsome head and frowned as he thought.

'Ah, yes, I remember. I didn't know it was the boathouse belonging to this house. If I'd known that, I would have tied up my boat there. When I asked how to get here, I was told to go to the quay.'

'I understand. But did you see anyone at the boathouse as you passed?'

'No. Why? Was someone there?'

'Well, Mr de Sousa, the girl was killed in the boathouse near the time when you were passing.'

'Ah. I see. You think I might have seen the crime. But why ask *me* in particular? There are plenty of boats going up and down. Why not ask them?'

'We *will* ask them,' said the Inspector, annoyed. Then he said, 'Lady Stubbs is a cousin of yours – yes?'

de Sousa shrugged.

'Yes, but not a close cousin. I haven't seen Hattie since she was fifteen.'

'And you thought you would come for a surprise visit?'

'Hardly a *surprise*, Inspector. I wrote to my cousin from France three weeks ago.'

The inspector was surprised.

'You wrote telling her you planned to visit her?'

'Yes. I told her I would probably arrive around this date, and would write again later.'

Inspector Bland looked hard at him. This was completely different from what he had been told about the arrival of Etienne de Sousa's letter at the breakfast table.

De Sousa looked back at him calmly.

'Did Lady Stubbs reply to your first letter?' the Inspector asked.

De Sousa paused before he answered.

'I don't think my cousin is very good at writing letters. She isn't very intelligent. However, I believe she has grown into a beautiful woman.'

'Haven't you seen her yet?'

De Sousa smiled.

'No. She seems to be missing,' he said.

'Mr de Sousa, is there any reason to believe that your cousin might be avoiding you?' Bland asked.

'Avoiding me? What a silly idea.'

Again the Inspector looked hard at de Sousa. What was going on under that calm appearance?

'I'll be here for two more days, Inspector, if you wish to ask me any more questions.'

He bowed politely and left.

'Now, where *is* that woman?' the Inspector said in a sharp voice.

'Seargent Cottrell is still searching the grounds, sir,' said Hoskins. 'But the gardener, who's taking the money at the entrance, says the lady hasn't left through the gate. There's also the path down to the quay, but the old man down there – Merdell, his name is – is sure she hasn't left that way. Then there's the top gate that leads over the fields to the youth hostel at Hoodown Park, but that's been locked because of trespassers, so she didn't go through there.'

'Perhaps that's right,' said the Inspector, 'but Sir George is still complaining about trespassers. If they can get in, she could get out the same way and go across the countryside.'

'Oh, yes, sir. But I've talked to people in the house. Lady Stubbs is wearing' – Hoskins looked at a notebook – 'a pink silk dress, a large hat, and shoes with very high heels. That isn't what you'd wear for running across the country.'

'She didn't change her clothes?'

'No. I asked, and there's nothing missing from her room. Not even shoes.'

Inspector Bland frowned.

'Get me that secretary woman again.'

He was starting to think about unpleasant possibilities.

Miss Brewis came in looking worried.

'Inspector, Sir George is very upset. He's realized Lady Stubbs is – well, really missing. He's worried that something's happened to her.'

'Well, Miss Brewis, we have had a murder here this afternoon.'

'But you don't think—? Oh that's impossible! Lady Stubbs can look after herself.'

'Really? Not everybody thinks so.'

Miss Brewis sighed. 'Oh, Lady Stubbs pretends that she can't do things for herself if she doesn't *want* to do something. Her husband believes it, I'm sure, but I don't!'

The door opened suddenly and Sir George came in.

'Now listen,' he said angrily, 'you've got to find Hattie. A maniac's somehow got into this fête, paying his money and looking like everyone else, and he's spending his afternoon going round murdering people—'

'Now, Sir George,' Inspector Bland said quietly.

'And you're just sitting there, writing things down. What I want is my wife.'

'My men are searching the grounds, Sir George.'

'Why did nobody tell me she'd disappeared? I thought it was strange she didn't come to judge the children's fancy dress contest, but nobody told me she'd really gone.'

'Nobody knew,' said the Inspector.

'Well, *somebody* should have noticed.'

He turned to Miss Brewis.

'You should have known, Amanda. You were in charge of things.'

'I can't be everywhere,' said Miss Brewis. Her voice was full of tears. 'If Lady Stubbs chose to walk off—'

'Walk off? She had no reason to walk off – unless she wanted to avoid that cousin of hers.'

Inspector Bland saw his opportunity.

'There is something I must ask you, sir. Did your wife receive a letter from Mr de Sousa three weeks ago, telling her he was coming?'

Sir George looked very surprised. 'No, of course she didn't. Hattie was completely startled and upset when she got his letter this morning. It gave her a big shock. She was lying down most of the morning with a headache.'

'What did she say to you about her cousin's visit? Why was she so afraid of seeing him?'

Sir George looked embarrassed.

'I really don't know,' he said. 'She just kept on repeating like a child that he was a wicked man. And she wished he wasn't coming. She said he'd done bad things.'

'When?'

'Oh, long ago. I imagine this Etienne de Sousa was the black sheep of the family[13] and Hattie heard things about him during her childhood without understanding them. So she's got a sort of fear of him from that time. My wife *does* behave like a child sometimes.'

'Did she give you any details, Sir George?'

Sir George looked unhappy. 'Well, I wouldn't want you to – er – believe everything that Hattie said...'

'Then she did say something?'

'All right. What she said – several times – was "*He kills people*."'

CHAPTER 10

'He kills people,' Inspector Bland repeated.

'Please don't think that it is a serious suggestion,' said Sir George. 'It was just some strange memory from her childhood. Anyway, it's not very likely that de Sousa arrives here in a yacht and immediately goes through the woods and kills a poor Girl Guide in a boathouse!'

'True,' said Inspector Bland, 'But, Sir George, our list of suspects for Marlene Tucker's murder is rather short.'

'Rather short!' Sir George said in surprise. 'You've got everybody at the fête to choose from.'

'No. The boathouse door was locked. Nobody could get in without a key.'

'Well, there were three keys.'

'Yes. One key was the final clue in this Murder Hunt. It's still hidden in the garden. Mrs Oliver had the second key. Where's the third key, Sir George?'

'In the drawer of that desk where you're sitting, with a lot of other keys for the estate.'

He came over and searched in the drawer. 'Yes. Here it is.'

'Then you see,' said Inspector Bland, 'the only people who could have got into the boathouse were Mrs Oliver, or someone who entered because *Marlene opened the door to them from the inside.* And for this Murder Hunt, when the girl heard anyone approaching the door she knew she had to lie down and be the victim, and wait to be discovered.

'So the only people she would have opened the door for *were the people who had arranged the Murder Hunt.*'

Sir George's face turned bright red.

'That's impossible! Absolutely impossible!'

'Sir George, we're doing all we can to find Lady Stubbs. Meanwhile, I'd like a chat with Mrs Legge and Michael Weyman.'

'I'll see what I can do, Inspector,' said Miss Brewis. She left the room with Sir George following her, calling after her in a sad voice.

'Amanda!'

At that moment, Inspector Bland thought that Sir George seemed rather like a young boy.

He picked up the telephone, called the police station, and arranged for the police to watch de Sousa's yacht.

◆ ◆ ◆

The door opened and a tall young man entered. He was wearing a grey suit, but his tie and his hair were very untidy.

'I'm Michael Weyman.'

Inspector Bland pointed to a chair.

'I don't like sitting,' said Weyman. 'I like to walk around. What are all you police doing here anyway? What's happened?'

Inspector Bland looked at him in surprise.

'I imagined all the people staying in the house would know what has happened by now. The girl who played the part of the murder victim has actually been killed.'

'No!' Weyman seemed very shocked. 'How?'

'She was strangled with a cord.'

Weyman made a noise of surprise.

'Just like in the Murder Hunt?' He walked over to the window and turned round. 'So now we're all murder suspects.'

The inspector paid no attention to that. Instead, he asked, 'You're here designing a tennis pavilion for Sir George – is that right?'

'Yes. It'll probably look awful,' said Michael, 'but that doesn't interest you, Inspector.'

'No. I'd like to know where you were this afternoon between a quarter past four and five o'clock.'

Instead of answering, Weyman asked: 'How did you decide on the time of death – was it a doctor's <u>evidence</u>?'

'Not completely, sir. Miss Brewis saw the girl alive at a quarter past four. Lady Stubbs asked her to take her some cakes.'

'Oh, I don't believe that. It's really not the sort of thing our Hattie would think of. Dear Lady Stubbs only thinks about herself.'

'I'm still waiting, Mr Weyman, for your answer to my question.'

'Well, really, Inspector, I was nearby. I mean, I chatted a bit with people on the lawn. Then I went along to the tennis court and thought about the design for the pavilion.'

'And after that?'

'I went down to the quay and had a talk with old Merdell, then I came back to the house.'

'And did you see Lady Stubbs during the afternoon?'

'Of course. Who could miss her? She was dressed like a fashion model. For some reason she likes people to think she's not very smart,' Weyman said, sounding a little angry, 'but she's really very clever.'

'I'd like to know if something has happened between him and Lady Stubbs,' said the Inspector after Weyman had left the room. 'What's the general opinion round here about Sir George and his lady?'

'Well, they say she's not very intelligent,' said Constable Hoskins.

'And Sir George – is he popular?'

'People like him, generally. He's good at sports and he knows a bit about farming. Mrs Folliat's done a lot to help him. She's introduced Sir George and his wife to all the most important people. She knew Lady Stubbs before she was married. It was Mrs Folliat who encouraged Sir George to buy this place.'

'I'll have to talk to Mrs Folliat,' said the Inspector.

'Ah, she's a clever old lady. If anything is going on, she'll know about it.'

◆ ◆ ◆

At that moment Mrs Folliat was with Hercule Poirot in the drawing room. He had found her sitting in a corner, holding a handkerchief, looking up at the ceiling. She said in a voice full of feeling:

'It's terrible to think of it. That poor girl. That poor, poor girl.'

'I know,' said Poirot. 'I know.'

'So young,' said Mrs Folliat, 'just at the beginning of her life.'

She seemed to have become ten years older, Poirot thought. She looked tired and ill.

'You said to me yesterday, Madame, that it is a wicked world.'

'It's true… Oh, yes, I'm only just beginning to know how true it is. But I never thought anything like this would happen.'

He looked at her in a curious way.

'But you did expect *something* to happen – something unusual.'

'No, no, Monsieur Poirot. I only mean it's not something you would expect to happen in the middle of a fête.'

Poirot continued.

'This morning, Sir George said that Lady Stubbs also mentioned the word "wicked".'

'Hattie did? Oh, don't speak of her to me – don't speak of her. I don't want to think about her.'

Poirot was very surprised that Mrs Folliat didn't want to talk about Hattie.

'You do know, Madame, that Lady Stubbs is missing? Do you think she might have run away because she has done something bad?'

'What are you trying to say, Monsieur Poirot?'

'I am saying that people who behave like children do not always understand what they are doing. If they suddenly become angry, they might even kill someone…'

Mrs Folliat suddenly became very angry.

'Hattie was never like that! I won't allow you to say things like that. She was a gentle, <u>warm-hearted</u> girl. Hattie would never have killed *anyone*.'

She faced him, breathing hard.

Suddenly, Constable Hoskins appeared and said to Mrs Folliat, 'The Inspector would be glad to have a chat with you.' Noting, as Poirot had done, that Mrs Folliat seemed very shocked, Hoskins added: 'if you feel well enough?'

'Of course I feel well enough.' Mrs Folliat stood up and followed Hoskins out of the room, looking like the confident owner of Nasse House again.

Poirot sat down and looked up at the ceiling, frowning.

'I think you may be able to help us, Mrs Folliat,' Inspector Bland said. 'You know the Tuckers, don't you?'

'Oh, yes, of course, they've always rented a cottage on the estate.'

'Then can you think of any reason why anyone would want to kill Marlene?'

'No. I just can't believe it, Inspector.'

'What about Lady Stubbs,' the Inspector asked. 'Could she have gone away because of an argument with her husband?'

'Oh, no, not at all,' said Mrs Folliat. 'The silly girl didn't want to meet this cousin of hers. So she's run away just like a child.'

'Nothing more than that?'

'Oh, no. I expect she'll come back again quite soon, feeling rather ashamed of herself.'

At that moment the door opened and an attractive woman with red hair came in.

'This is Mrs Legge, Inspector,' said Mrs Folliat. 'Sally, have you heard about the terrible thing that's happened?'

'Oh, yes! Awful, isn't it?' said Mrs Legge. She sat down in a chair.

'I just can't believe it and I'm really sorry I can't help you, Inspector,' she said. 'You see, I've been in the fortune-telling tent all afternoon, so I haven't seen anything of what was going on.'

The Inspector nodded. 'But you do understand we have to ask everybody the same questions? Mrs Legge, where were you between four-fifteen and five o'clock?'

'Well, I went and had tea at four. I hung a card up outside the tent: *Back at 4.30*. The tea tent was really crowded but I managed to get back on time.'

'When did you last see Lady Stubbs?'

'Hattie? She was near the tent when I went to tea, but I don't remember seeing her afterwards. Is it true she's missing?'

'Yes, it is.'

'Oh, well,' said Sally Legge not seeming very worried, 'she's not very intelligent, you know. I expect that having a murder here has frightened her.'

♦ ♦ ♦

Hercule Poirot and Inspector Bland were discussing what they knew. They agreed that, so far, the facts had not led them to any conclusion. They looked at one another across the desk.

'But what do you think?' Poirot asked.

'That we have a lot of work to do, that's clear. And I think,' said the Inspector seriously, 'that Marlene Tucker saw something she was not meant to see, and because of that she was killed.'

'I will not disagree with you,' said Poirot.

'She might have seen a murder,' said the inspector. Then: 'What do *you* think, Poirot? Is Lady Stubbs alive or dead?'

Poirot paused for a moment before he replied.

'I think, my friend, that Lady Stubbs is dead. And I believe that Mrs Folliat knows a lot more than we do.'

♦ ♦ ♦

The following morning, Hercule Poirot went out into the garden and into the fortune-telling tent where Madame Zuleika had sat.

It was a conversation between Sally Legge and Captain Warburton that led him here. Mrs Legge had said that everyone had agreed the fortune-telling tent should be on this side of the lawn. Had it been, he wondered, one of those moments of which

Mrs Oliver had spoken? "One person working through other people who don't know that anything is going on."

In addition, thought Poirot, there was the fact that Mrs Legge had been without visitors between four o'clock and half past four. She said she had been in the tea tent, but it was so busy there was no one who could say if that was true. Could she have used her tea break to go out the back of her tent and murder Marlene? What reason would she have?

Poirot opened the tent at the back, stepped out and walked through the bushes behind. He soon reached a small, old summerhouse.

Very little light came in through the bushes but he could just see an almost round mark in the dust on the floor.

Poirot looked at it for a long time. He felt that if he could understand this, then many other things would become clear. But he didn't understand it!

At last Poirot went out and found the path to the folly.

As he walked, he felt a need to consider every bush as a possible place for hiding a body.

He came at last to the folly and, going inside, he sat down to rest his feet.

Through the trees he could just see the river. He found himself agreeing with Michael Weyman, the young architect, that this was not a good place to put a folly. There was no view.

It was the same with his thoughts – he just couldn't get a clear view of the facts. The whole thing must tie together into some kind of pattern, but how?

Poirot continued down the path to the boathouse. He had the key so he went inside.

It was as he remembered, except that the body and the tea tray had been taken away. On the table where the magazines still lay, he noted some words that Marlene had written on them. *Jack Blake goes with Susan Brown. Peter takes girls to the cinema.*

He remembered Marlene's face. She was not a pretty girl. He suspected that boys had never taken Marlene to the cinema. So Marlene enjoyed spying on people. She had seen things she was not meant to see – things of small importance. But perhaps she had once seen something of more importance...

But what?

Poirot went slowly out of the boathouse, unhappy with himself. He, Hercule Poirot, had been brought here to prevent a murder – and he had *not* prevented it. What was even more embarrassing was that he had no real ideas about what had actually happened.

He must return to London without solving the crime.

CHAPTER 12

Hercule Poirot sat in a square chair in front of a square table in the square room of his London flat.

He sighed. He looked at the chair on the other side of the table. There, less than half an hour ago, Inspector Bland had sat, having tea and cakes and talking with great disappointment.

He had come to London on police business and then visited Monsieur Poirot. He wondered, he had said, if Poirot had any new ideas about the murder at Nasse House.

It was now nearly five weeks since the crime had happened – five weeks with no progress. Lady Stubbs' body had not been found. If she was still alive, nobody knew where she had gone. However, Inspector Bland said, it was very unlikely that she was still alive.

Poirot agreed.

'Of course,' said Bland, 'if her body was put in the river, perhaps it was carried out to sea.'

'I have another idea,' Poirot said, and explained.

Bland nodded.

'You mean the body is at Nasse, hidden somewhere we never thought of looking. It could be. With an old house and grounds like that, there are places you'd never know were there.'

'The person who would know,' said Poirot, 'is Mrs Folliat.'

Mrs Folliat, thought Poirot, was in the middle of the whole thing. He just didn't know why or how yet.

'I've interviewed the lady several times,' said the Inspector. 'She's very nice, very upset and can't suggest anything helpful.'

'Can't or won't?' thought Poirot to himself. Bland was perhaps thinking the same.

The Inspector finished his tea, sighed and left.

Poirot felt angry and embarrassed. Mrs Oliver had asked him, Hercule Poirot, to come to Devon to help, and he had not succeeded. He was in a fog where sometimes a pale light shone through, but he didn't understand the light.

'I know a lot of things,' said Hercule Poirot to himself. 'But I am not looking at them all the right way.'

Poirot took a notebook from his pocket and wrote:

Did Lady Stubbs really ask Miss Brewis to take tea to Marlene? If not, why does Miss Brewis say that she did?

He thought about it. Why would Miss Brewis lie about that? He wrote down something more.

Etienne de Sousa says that he wrote to his cousin three weeks before his arrival at Nasse House. Is that true or false?

Poirot felt these questions were very important to discovering the truth.

But he could not think of any reason why Sir George or Lady Stubbs would pretend to be surprised or upset when the second letter arrived. And if Etienne de Sousa had lied about the first letter, *why* did he lie?

Hercule Poirot brought his hand down suddenly on his chair. He had made a decision.

'I can no longer sit and think. No, I must go back to Devon and visit Mrs Folliat again.'

◆ ◆ ◆

Hercule Poirot paused at the gates of Nasse House. It was a sunny afternoon but it was no longer summer. Along the drive, there were golden-brown leaves which had fallen from the trees.

Poirot knocked at the door of the Lodge. He heard someone coming slowly, then the door opened. He was startled to see how old and thin Mrs Folliat looked. She looked at him, shocked:

'Monsieur Poirot? It's you!'

He thought for a moment he had seen fear appear in her eyes.

'May I come in, Madame?'

'Well, of course.'

She became calm again and led him into her small sitting room. There were already some tea things on a table. Mrs Folliat said:

'I'll just fetch another cup.'

Poirot looked round. Against the wall was a bookcase – and an old photograph in a silver frame of a man in a soldier's uniform.

Mrs Folliat came back with a cup and saucer.

Poirot pointed to the photograph, 'Your husband, Madame?'

'Yes.' She continued quickly, 'I'm not fond of photographs. They make one live too much in the past. One must learn to forget, to cut out the dead wood.'

Poirot remembered the first time he had seen her – she had been gardening up at the house. She was, he thought, a woman who could be cruel. One who could cut out dead wood not only from her plants and bushes but also from her life...

She handed him his tea.

'Has there been any news of Lady Stubbs?' Poirot asked.

Mrs Folliat shook her head slowly.

'I think George has given up hoping that his wife is alive, though I haven't seen him recently; he's mostly been in London.'

'And the murdered girl? There has been no progress?'

'I haven't heard.' She added, 'It seems to be a crime absolutely without reason. Poor child...'

'You are still upset about it, Madame.'

Mrs Folliat didn't reply for a moment or two. Then she said:

'I think, when you get old, the death of someone young seems more terrible than anything else. We old people expect to die, but that child had her whole life in front of her.'

'Although we expect to die,' said Poirot, 'we do not want to. At least *I* do not. I still find life very interesting.'

'Oh, I don't.' She looked even more tired. 'I'm exhausted, Monsieur Poirot. I'll be ready when my time to die comes.'

He wondered about the reason for this great tiredness. He felt that Amy Folliat was a very strong woman. She had lived through many troubles and cut out the 'dead wood'. But there was something now in her life that she could not cut out.

'Really, I don't have much to live for, Monsieur Poirot.' she said, reading his thoughts. 'I have many friends but no family.'

'You have your home,' said Poirot suddenly.

'You mean Nasse? Yes.'

'It is still *your* home, is it not, although Sir George Stubbs is the owner? Now that Sir George has gone to London, you have control of it.'

Again he saw the sharp look of fear in her eyes. Her voice now was icy cold.

'I don't know what you mean, Monsieur Poirot. I'm grateful to Sir George for renting me the Lodge, but I *do* rent it. I pay him money once a year, for which he also allows me to walk in the grounds.'

Poirot moved more closely towards her.

'Madame, you know *who* killed Marlene Tucker, and you know *why*. You also know who killed Hattie Stubbs, and where her body lies now.'

Mrs Folliat's voice was loud and hard. 'I know nothing. *Nothing.*'

'Perhaps I have used the wrong word, Madame. You do not know but you suspect—'

'I suspect nothing.'

'That is not true, Madame.'

'Well, it would be wrong to speak only because I *suspect* something wicked.'

'As wrong as what was done here?' Poirot asked.

She moved back into her chair as far as possible, and said very quietly:

'Don't talk to me of it. It's over. Finished.'

'Madame. It is *never* finished with a murderer.'

She shook her head.

'No. No, it's the end. And there is nothing *I* can do. Nothing.'

CHAPTER 13

Poirot found the cottage where the Tuckers lived, and knocked on the door.

'Marilyn, there's someone at the door. Go and see who it is,' called Mrs Tucker in a high voice.

The door was opened and a fat child of about twelve looked out at Poirot. She was a pretty girl with blue eyes.

Then Mrs Tucker came to the door with bits of hair hanging over her face.

'What is it?' she demanded in a sharp voice. Then she recognized Poirot. 'Weren't you with the police that day?'

'I am very sorry, Madame, that I have brought back sad memories,' said Poirot.

'Come in, sir,' she said, opening a door on her right. Poirot stepped inside the cottage and was taken into a neat little sitting room.

It contained a sofa and chairs, a round table, and some flowers in pots.

'Sit down, sir, please. I don't think I know your name.'

'My name is Hercule Poirot,' said Poirot. 'I called to tell you how sorry I am about what happened. I also wanted to ask if there had been any progress with solving the crime.'

'No – nobody has seen or heard anything about the murderer,' said Mrs Tucker, angrily. 'It's terrible. It's my opinion that the police don't try very hard when ordinary people like us are the victims of crime.'

Just then, Mr Tucker appeared at the door. He was a large, red-faced man with a calm face.

'The police are doing their job,' he said. 'They've got their challenges like everyone else. These maniacs aren't easy to find. They look the same as you or me,' he added, speaking to Poirot.

The little girl who had opened the door appeared behind her father and looked at Poirot with great interest.

'It's very nice of you, sir,' said Mr Tucker, 'to come and ask about Marlene.'

'I have been wondering whether Marlene already knew this – er – maniac.'

'No, she wouldn't know anybody like that,' said Mrs Tucker.

'Ah,' said Poirot, 'but someone may have made friends with Marlene without you knowing. Perhaps they gave her presents.'

'Oh, no, sir, Marlene wouldn't take presents from a stranger. I taught her not to do that.'

'But she might not think there was anything wrong with it,' said Poirot. 'For example, if a nice lady had offered her things.'

'Like Mrs Legge? She gave Marlene some make-up once,' said Mrs Tucker. 'I was very angry. "I'm not going to let you put that on your face, Marlene," I said. "Not until you're much older."'

'But she did not agree with you – is that right?' said Poirot, smiling.

Young Marilyn laughed. Poirot glanced at her.

'Did Mrs Legge give Marlene anything else?' he asked.

'Yes, a scarf – a brightly coloured thing. Young girls like nice things,' said Mrs Tucker. 'But I wasn't happy about that either.'

Mrs Tucker continued: 'So I was a bit sharp with her.' Tears came into her eyes. 'And now she's been killed in that terrible way. I wished afterwards I hadn't spoken in such a sharp way. We've had only trouble and death recently.'

'Have you also lost someone else?' asked Poirot politely.

'My wife's father,' explained Mr Tucker. 'He was crossing the river in his boat late at night, and must have slipped getting onto the quay. He fell in the river. He was always doing things on the quay.'

'Father loved being around boats,' said Mrs Tucker. 'He used to look after them for Mr Folliat when he was still here.'

Poirot was remembering something.

'An old man – on the quay? Yes, I remember talking to him. Was his name—?'

'Merdell, sir. That was my name before I married.'

'Your father, if I remember correctly, was head gardener at Nasse?'

'No, that was his son – my oldest brother.' She added proudly, 'There have been Merdells at Nasse for years. But they've all left and gone to other places now. Father was the last.'

Poirot said quietly:

'There'll always be Folliats at Nasse.'

'Pardon, sir?'

'I am repeating what your father said to me on the quay.'

'Ah, he said a lot of silly things.'

'So Marlene was Merdell's granddaughter,' said Poirot. 'Yes, I am beginning to understand.' Suddenly he began to feel very excited. 'Your father fell into the river, you say?'

'Yes, sir. He slipped and fell in. It's surprising it never happened before – he was ninety-two.'

'But it did *not* happen before,' Poirot got up. 'I should have guessed long ago. Marlene almost told me—'

'Pardon, sir?'

'It is nothing,' said Poirot. 'Once more I am very sorry, about the death of both your daughter and your father.'

He shook hands with them and left the cottage. He said to himself: 'I have been very stupid. I have looked at everything the wrong way round.'

'Hey, there.'

Poirot heard a voice. He looked around. The child Marilyn was standing in the shadow of the cottage wall. He walked over to her. She spoke very quietly.

'Mum doesn't know everything. Marlene didn't get that scarf from Mrs Legge.'

'Where did she get it?'

'She bought it in Torquay. She bought some make-up, too, and some perfume.' Marilyn laughed. 'Mum doesn't know. Marlene hid it all at the back of her drawer, under her underwear.'

Marilyn laughed again.

'I've got it all now – in *my* drawer.'

Poirot looked at her carefully. 'You seem like a very clever girl, Marilyn. Tell me, how did Marlene get the money to buy these things?'

Marilyn looked down at the ground. 'I don't know.'

Poirot took out a coin and then another. 'I think you do know.'

Marilyn's hand moved towards the money. She spoke very quickly and quietly. 'Marlene used to spy on people. She used to see things she shouldn't have seen. Marlene would promise not to tell and then they'd give her a present.'

Poirot gave her the coins. 'I see.'

He nodded and walked away.

He now understood so many things. Everything had been very clear but he had not been smart enough to see it.

Poirot called Inspector Bland.

'I have a question,' Poirot said. 'What kind of a yacht did Etienne de Sousa have?'

'Ah, Monsieur Poirot, we searched it. There was nowhere you could hide a body. And no evidence that he knew the Girl Guide.'

'No, no, that is not what I mean. Was it big or small?'

'Oh, it was very expensive. It must have cost a lot of money.'

'That is right,' said Poirot, with great pleasure. 'Etienne de Sousa and his family are rich. That, my friend, is very important.'

'Why?' demanded Inspector Bland.

But Poirot had already put down the phone. Next he called Mrs Oliver.

'I'm delighted that you've called,' Mrs Oliver said. 'I was just going out to give a talk on *How I Write My Books*. Now I can get my secretary to say that something has happened and I can't come.'

'But, Madame, you must not let me prevent—'

'You haven't prevented anything,' said Mrs Oliver happily. 'I mean, what *can* you say about how you write books? I mean, first you've got to think of something, then you've got to make yourself sit down and write it. That's all. It would take three minutes to explain that, then the talk would have ended and everyone would have been disappointed.'

'But *I* want to ask you about how you write.'

'You can ask,' said Mrs Oliver, 'but I probably won't know the answer. I mean, I just write. Just a moment, I've got a very silly hat on for the talk and I *must* take it off. It hurts my forehead.' There was a pause and then she returned. 'That's better. Hats don't really mean anything these days, do they? I mean, people don't wear them for sensible reasons any more; to keep their head warm, or hide their face from people they don't want to meet.'

'Ahah! It is extraordinary,' said Poirot, with his voice full of respect. 'You always give me ideas. You have given me now an answer. But anyway, let me ask you my question. Sally Legge's husband is a scientist, yes?'

'Yes.'

'Is he an atomic scientist?'

'Yes, I think he is. Why?'

'Then I believe that when you met Mrs Legge at Nasse House, it probably put the idea of an atomic scientist into your head. You get ideas for the characters in your books from the people you meet in real life. But his wife is not Yugoslavian.'

'Oh, *no*,' said Mrs Oliver, 'Sally's English.'

'Then what put the idea of the Yugoslavian wife into your head?'

'I don't know... Students, perhaps? All those foreign girls at the hostel trespassing through the woods?'

'I see... Yes, I see now a lot of things.'

'At long last,' said Mrs Oliver.

'Excuse me?'

'I said at long last. Up to now you haven't done *anything*.' There was disappointment in her voice. 'And meanwhile there have been two murders.'

'Three,' Poirot said.

'Three? Who's the third?'

'An old man called Merdell,' said Poirot. 'But there is more I must ask you. When you first began to plan your Murder Hunt, did you want the body to be in the boathouse?'

'No, it was going to be in that funny little summerhouse hidden in the bushes near the house. But then someone began insisting it should be found in the folly. That, of course, was *silly*! I mean, anyone could have walked in there and found the body without following any of the clues. Of course I couldn't agree to *that*.'

'So, instead, you accepted the boathouse?'

'Yes.'

'And that is just what you told me on the day I arrived – you agreed to small changes because you did not want to accept larger ones. That is very interesting.'

◆ ◆ ◆

Inspector Bland looked up in a curious way as Hercule Poirot entered his office.

'So here you are, Monsieur Poirot.' They shook hands. 'I'm keen to hear this *evidence* you have.'

'Yes indeed, Inspector. The evidence is Lady Stubbs' body. *I know where it is hidden.* You must go to the place and *then* you will have all the evidence you need. There is only one person who could have hidden it there.'

'And who's that?'

Hercule Poirot smiled – the happy smile of a cat that has just drunk a saucer of cream.

'The person it so often is,' he said in a soft voice. 'The *husband*. Sir George Stubbs killed his wife.'

'But that's impossible, Monsieur Poirot. We *know* it's impossible. He was at the fête all day.'

'Oh, no,' said Poirot, 'it is not impossible at all! Listen, and I will tell you...'

Chapter 14

Along the drive, the last golden-brown leaves had fallen from the trees long ago.

Hercule Poirot sighed and knocked gently on the door of the Lodge.

He heard someone coming slowly to the door. It was opened by Mrs Folliat.

'Monsieur Poirot! You again?'

'May I come in?'

'Of course.'

She offered him tea, which he refused. Then she asked quietly: 'Why have you come?'

'I think you can guess, Madame. There have now been three deaths, Hattie Stubbs, Marlene Tucker, and old Merdell.'

She said in a sharp voice: 'Merdell? That was an accident. He fell from the quay.'

'Actually, it was not an accident. Merdell knew too much. He recognized a face, or a voice – something like that. On that first day he told me about the Folliat family – about your sons who were killed in the war. But they were not *both* killed, were they? Your second son, James, ran away from the Army. It was reported that he was 'missing, believed killed', and later you told everyone he *was* killed. But that was not true – your son is alive.'

Poirot paused.

'I do understand something about how you feel, Madame. You knew what your younger son was like – a difficult boy – but he *was* your son, and you loved him. So you did everything you could to give him a new life. You *created* Sir George Stubbs. You were in charge of a rich young girl who was not very intelligent. Oh yes, she was rich. You pretended that her family had become poor but that was not true. I realised this when I met Etienne de Sousa – how could he have such money and poor Hattie's side of the family have nothing at all? Oh no, Hattie's family had money – a lot of money. In fact, you knew that when she married, she would receive full control of her family's money. So you arranged for her to marry Sir George.

'She was, as you told me, very easy to influence. She signed all the documents her husband asked her to sign. It was very quick and easy for Sir George Stubbs to become a rich man while his wife became very poor.

'So the rich Sir George Stubbs, older and with a new beard, bought Nasse House and came to live where he belonged. He had not been there since he was a boy and there was nobody left after the war to recognize him – except old Merdell. And when he said to me that *there would always be Folliats at Nasse*, that was his private joke.

'So everything had turned out well. Your plan, I believe, ended there. Your son was very rich, he was back in his family home, and he had a beautiful wife. You hoped he would be kind to her and she would be happy.'

Mrs Folliat said in a quiet voice:

'That's how I thought it would be – *I* would look after Hattie and care for her. I never imagined—'

'You never imagined – and your son did not tell you – that *he was already married*. Oh, yes – we have seen the documents. Your son had married a girl who was a criminal in Trieste, where he had hidden after he ran away from the Army. They never intended to leave each other. He accepted the marriage with Hattie as a way to get rich, but he knew from the beginning what he intended to do.'

'No, no! I cannot believe that... It was *her* — *that wicked woman*—'

Poirot continued:

'*He intended to murder Hattie from the moment he agreed to the marriage.* When he had all her money he brought Hattie across to England from France, and he brought her straight here to Nasse. But nobody saw her very much that first evening because he took her straight to her bedroom. *The woman the staff saw the next morning at breakfast was not Hattie.* She was his Italian wife wearing Hattie's clothes and make-up, and behaving as Hattie behaved. The real Hattie was already dead.

'Over the years I'm sure the false Hattie's problems would have improved because of "new ways of dealing with problems of the mind." In fact, Miss Brewis already realized there was not much wrong with Lady Stubbs' mind. But she was no danger, and it might all have ended there.

'But then a cousin of Hattie's wrote that he was coming to England in his yacht. Of course he would recognize that 'Hattie' was false. And there was another problem — old Merdell used to chat to his granddaughter, Marlene. She did not know whether to believe him, but she told Sir George about some of the things he said — for example, that he had seen "a woman's body in the woods," and perhaps that "Sir George Stubbs was really Mr James". So Sir George decided to kill her. I imagine he gave her small amounts of money while he made his plans.

'They worked out their plan very carefully. Marlene would be killed and Lady Stubbs would "disappear" in a way that would make people suspect de Sousa. That was why he was described as a "wicked man" who "kills people".

'Hattie Stubbs was meant to disappear forever; Sir George's first Italian wife would then be able to take her place. All she needed to do was to play both parts for just over twenty-four hours. Well, that was easy. On the day I arrived, Mrs Folliat said that "Lady Stubbs" had remained in her room until teatime. Actually, she left the house quietly, took a train to Exeter, and travelled from Exeter with another young girl. She arrived at the hostel, reserved her bed, and went out to *"explore"*, which is when she returned to Nasse House. By teatime, "Lady Stubbs" was in the drawing room.

'After dinner, she went to bed – but really she left the house and spent the night in the hostel so that the girl she had travelled with did not miss her. She was back at Nasse House as Lady Stubbs in time for breakfast. Again she spent the morning in her room with a "headache". This time the Italian girl appeared before the fête began, as a "trespasser". She was sent away by Sir George from the window of his wife's room where he *pretended* to turn and speak to his wife inside.

'The changes of clothes were not difficult – shorts and a shirt could be hidden under one of the big expensive dresses Lady Stubbs was fond of wearing. The travelling Italian girl wore a bright headscarf, and her face was brown from the sun; Hattie had a lot of white make-up with a big hat, allowing her to hide her face. No one even imagined that those two could be the same woman.

'And so the final event in the story began. Just before four o'clock "Lady Stubbs" told Miss Brewis to take a tea tray down to Marlene in the boathouse. The plan would all go wrong if Miss Brewis thought of that by herself, and appeared in the boathouse at the wrong moment. So they made sure it happened *before* the planned time of the murder. Then "Lady Stubbs" went quietly into the empty fortune-telling tent (Sally Legge was having tea at 4 pm), out through the back and into the summerhouse.

She had left a rucksack there with a change of clothes – I found a round mark on the floor which, I now realise, was from this rucksack. She took the rucksack, went through the woods to the boathouse, called to Marlene to let her in, and strangled her. She changed her clothes and make-up, and packed the dress and shoes in the rucksack. Soon afterwards, dressed as the Italian student from the youth hostel, she joined her Dutch friend on the lawn, and left with her by the local bus. I suspect she is in London now. Wherever she is, it does not matter – the police are looking for Hattie Stubbs, not an Italian girl.

'But poor Hattie Stubbs is dead, as you know very well, Madame. She has been dead for some time.

'The death of Marlene was a bad shock to you – you had no idea what your son had planned. But on the day of the fete, you told me very clearly that Hattie was dead, though I was too stupid to see it at the time. When you talked about "Hattie", you were talking about *two different people*. One was a woman you disliked: "Don't speak of her. I don't want to think about her." The other was a girl you spoke of in the past tense. You defended that girl. You said: "Hattie was never like that! She was a gentle, warm-hearted girl."

'I think, Madame, that you were very fond of poor Hattie Stubbs.'

He paused.

Mrs Folliat sat without moving. At last she spoke. Her voice was cold as ice.

'Your story is completely false, Monsieur Poirot. I think you must be mad. All this is completely in your head; you have no evidence at all.'

Poirot went across to one of the windows and opened it.

'Listen, Madame. What do you hear?'

'I'm a little deaf... What should I hear?'

'The police are breaking up the concrete floor of the folly. What a good place to bury a body – where a tree has fallen over and the ground is easy to dig. And to make everything safe, build a folly on top...'

He added gently: 'Sir George's folly... The folly of the owner of Nasse House.'

He paused.

'It is such a beautiful place,' said Poirot. 'There is only one bad thing – the man who owns it...'

Mrs Folliat sighed.

'I know,' said Mrs Folliat in a low voice. 'I've always known... Even as a child he frightened me... He was very cruel and never sorry about the bad things he did. But he was my son and I loved him.

'I should have gone to the police after Hattie's death... But he was my son. How could I tell them? And now, because I didn't say anything, that poor silly child was killed... And after her, old Merdell... Where would it have ended?'

'With a murderer it does not end,' said Poirot.

She looked down at the ground. For a moment or two she stayed like that, her hands covering her eyes.

Then Mrs Folliat of Nasse House, daughter of a long line of brave men, sat up, her back straight. She looked at Poirot and her voice was cold and came from far away.

'Thank you, Monsieur Poirot,' she said, 'for coming to tell me yourself about this. Will you leave me now? I think I need to be alone...'

◆ CHARACTER LIST ◆

Miss Lemon: secretary to Hercule Poirot

Hercule Poirot: a very famous Belgian policeman, now retired, who has lived in England for many years working as a private detective

Mrs Ariadne Oliver: a famous crime writer

Sir George Stubbs: a rich businessman, owner of Nasse House

Lady Hattie Stubbs: Sir George's wife

Michael Weyman: an architect working for Sir George Stubbs

Miss Amanda Brewis: secretary to Sir George Stubbs

Mrs Sally Legge: a young lady who lives nearby with her husband and helps with the fête at Nasse House

Mrs Masterton: wife of the local Member of Parliament, also helping with the fête at Nasse House

Jim Warburton: political agent to Mrs Masterton's husband

Mrs Amy Folliat: elderly lady whose family owned Nasse House until recently

Marlene Tucker: 14-year-old Girl Guide

Etienne de Sousa: cousin of Hattie Stubbs

Inspector Bland: a member of the Devonshire Police

Constable Robert Hoskins: a local policeman

Mr and Mrs Tucker: Marlene's father and mother

Marilyn Tucker: Marlene's younger sister

Merdell: an old man who works down at the quay

1. Devon

An area in south-west England (see map below). Devon is a popular place for tourists to visit, especially in the summer. It offers many things for visitors to see and do, such as walking, sailing and enjoying the beautiful countryside. It has sandy beaches, many pretty villages and a large national park called Dartmoor, where you can see a variety of interesting wildlife. There are several historic cities and towns in Devon which attract many visitors every year. The most famous of these are Exeter, and Plymouth and Torquay on the coast.

2. Telephones

When this story was written (in 1956) people did not have mobile phones, or house telephones without a <u>cord</u> that you could carry from one room to another. Not every house in Britain had a telephone, and some houses had to share telephone lines. In houses that did have a telephone, there was usually only one, which was placed in a room like the hall where everyone could use it. This is why Mrs Oliver tells Poirot she can't talk – people could hear her conversation.

3. Youth hostels

At the time the story was written (in 1956), youth hostels were a very new idea. Today it is very normal for young people to travel to different countries. When travelling, many stay in youth hostels because they offer good but cheap accommodation for short periods. However, at the time of *Dead Man's Folly*, travelling was much more of an adventure for young people, especially as they had no mobile phones or internet to help them plan and to stay in contact with people at home.

In addition, many people living in towns and villages in Britain were not used to meeting young people from different cultures. It was a new and interesting thing.

4. Sir, Lady and social class

At the time of the story, British society was divided into different levels. People in the top level were usually called by a special word in front of their name to show their high position, for example, **Sir** for a man, and **Lady** for a woman. The highest level of society included the **landed gentry**, families who had owned large estates for centuries. The Folliat family in the story belongs to this group.

5. Folly

This word has two meanings. Both are used in the story to make a 'play on words.' The first meaning is a small tower or other kind of unusual building in a large garden or park. Follies were usually white, had no real purpose, and were very expensive to build. However, they were often popular with rich people as a way to decorate their large gardens.

The second meaning of **folly** is an action that is silly, or not sensible.

6. Member of Parliament (MP)

The UK is divided into political areas, and a Member of Parliament (MP) is a person chosen to be a member of the government by the people living in that area. The MP listens to the political views of the people who have chosen him or her and acts for them when the government is making decisions, for example, when the laws of the country are being made or changed.

In the story, Mr Masterton, the local MP, has a **political agent**, Jim Warburton, whose job is to help him and to organize political events.

7. Gate lodges

A gate lodge is a small house that was built at the gates of a big house. They were often lived in by the gardener or another person who worked for the owners of the big house.

In this story Mrs Folliat, who used to own Nasse House, now rents the gate lodge (known simply as 'the Lodge'). This is an unusual situation, but it suits her well because she can continue to enjoy the grounds and to work in the gardens.

8. Death duties

At the time of the story, death duties were a tax that had to be paid to the British government on the money and property of someone who had died. The tax still exists but the name was changed in 1975 to inheritance tax.

9. Girl Guides

An organization for girls, now called the Guides. In this organization, girls learn a variety of useful life skills. These help them to become independent, useful members of society while also enjoying themselves and having fun with activities like camping.

10. The Admiralty

The government department that is in charge of the <u>Navy</u>.

11. The Second World War

The Second World War, or World War II, was from 1939–1945, so it ended around 10 years before this story was written.

12. Police ranks

There are lots of different levels of jobs in the British police organization. Of the three levels, **Inspector** is the highest, **Sergeant** is in the middle, and **Constable** is the lowest.

13. The black sheep of the family

The black sheep of a group or family is a person the other members of the group think is different from the others, usually in a bad way.

◆ Glossary ◆

atomic scientist COUNTABLE NOUN
An **atomic scientist** is someone who has studied atoms and the power produced by splitting them. An atom is the smallest part of a something.

boathouse COUNTABLE NOUN
A **boathouse** is a building at the edge of a lake or river where boats are kept.

bow INTRANSITIVE VERB
When you **bow** to someone, you briefly move the top half of your body towards them and down as a formal way of greeting them.

bush COUNTABLE NOUN
A **bush** is a plant which is like a very small tree.

butler COUNTABLE NOUN
A **butler** is the chief male member of staff in the house of a wealthy family.

clue COUNTABLE NOUN
A **clue** to a problem or mystery is something that helps you find the answer.

concrete UNCOUNTABLE NOUN
Concrete is used for building, and is made from cement, sand, small stones, and water.

cord VARIABLE NOUN
Cord is strong thick string.

dramatic ADJECTIVE
If you say that someone is being **dramatic**, you mean they are showing their feelings in an obvious way because they want you to notice them.

drawing room COUNTABLE NOUN
A **drawing room** is a room, especially a large room in a large house, where people sit and relax, or talk to guests.

drive COUNTABLE NOUN
A **drive** is a private road leading from a public road to a house.

emerald COUNTABLE NOUN
An **emerald** is a bright green precious stone.

estate COUNTABLE NOUN
An **estate** is a large area of land in the country owned by one person or organization.

evidence UNCOUNTABLE NOUN
Evidence is information which is used to prove something.

fancy dress UNCOUNTABLE NOUN
Fancy dress is clothing that you wear for a party at which everyone tries to look like a famous person or a person from a story.

fence UNCOUNTABLE NOUN
A **fence** is something between two areas of land that stops people or animals moving between the two areas. It is usually made of wood or thin metal.

fête COUNTABLE NOUN
A **fête** is an event held outdoors that includes competitions and where home-made goods are sold.

folly COUNTABLE NOUN
A **folly** is a small building that was built as a decoration in a large garden or park, especially in Britain in the past.
VARIABLE NOUN
If you say that something is a **folly**, you mean that it is foolish.

fortune-telling UNCOUNTABLE NOUN
If someone does **fortune-telling**, they tell you what they think will happen to you in the future, after looking at something such as the lines on your hand.

frown INTRANSITIVE VERB
If you **frown**, you move your eyebrows close together because you are annoyed, worried, or thinking hard.

gardener COUNTABLE NOUN
A **gardener** is a person who is paid to work in someone else's garden.

grounds PLURAL NOUN
The **grounds** of a large or important building are the garden or area of land which surrounds it.

handkerchief COUNTABLE NOUN
A **handkerchief** is a small square of material which you use for blowing your nose.

headscarf COUNTABLE NOUN
A **headscarf** is a small square scarf which some women wear round their heads, for example to keep their hair tidy.

influence TRANSITIVE VERB
If you **influence** someone, you use your power to make them agree with you or do what you want.

judge TRANSITIVE VERB
If you **judge** a competition, you decide who the winner is.

lawn VARIABLE NOUN
A **lawn** is an area of grass that is kept cut short and is usually part of a garden or park.

leaflet COUNTABLE NOUN
A **leaflet** is a little book or a piece of paper containing information about a particular subject.

maniac COUNTABLE NOUN
A **maniac** is a mad person who is dangerous and hurts other people.

mark COUNTABLE NOUN
A **mark** is a small area of something, such as dirt, that has got onto something else.

motive COUNTABLE NOUN
Your **motive** for doing something is your reason for doing it.

Navy COUNTABLE NOUN
A country's **Navy** is the part of its armed forces that fights at sea.

nod INTRANSITIVE VERB
If you **nod** , you move your head down and up to show agreement, understanding, or approval.

pavilion COUNTABLE NOUN
A **pavilion** is a building on the edge of a sports field where players can change their clothes and wash.

poison VARIABLE NOUN
Poison harms or kills people or animals if they swallow it.

pretend TRANSITIVE VERB
If you **pretend** that something is true, you try to make people believe that it is true, although it is not.

quay COUNTABLE NOUN
A **quay** is a place beside the sea or a river where boats can be tied.

rucksack COUNTABLE NOUN
A **rucksack** is a bag which is used for carrying things on your back.

search TRANSITIVE VERB
If you **search** a place, you look carefully for someone or something there.

secret agent COUNTABLE NOUN
A **secret agent** is a person who is employed by a government to find out the secrets of other governments.

shake TRANSITIVE VERB
If you **shake** your head, you move it from side to side in order to say 'no'.
INTRANSITIVE VERB
If your voice **shakes**, it sounds very weak, for example because you are nervous or upset.

shrug INTRANSITIVE VERB
If you **shrug** , you raise your shoulders to show that you are not interested in something or that you do not know something.

sigh INTRANSITIVE VERB
When you **sigh**, you breathe out slowly making a noise.

spy INTRANSITIVE VERB
If you **spy** on someone, you watch them secretly.

squire COUNTABLE NOUN
In the past, the **squire** of an English village was the man who owned most of the land in it.

stab TRANSITIVE VERB
If someone **stabs** another person, they push a knife into their body.

startled ADJECTIVE
If you are **startled** , you are surprised and slightly frightened.

strangle TRANSITIVE VERB
To **strangle** someone means to kill them by pressing on their throat.

summerhouse COUNTABLE NOUN
A **summerhouse** is a small building in a garden which has seats so that people can sit there in the summer.

suspect COUNTABLE NOUN
A **suspect** is a person who the police think may be guilty of a crime.
TRANSITIVE VERB
If you say that you **suspect** that something is true, you mean that you believe that it is probably true, but you want to make it sound less strong.

terrace COUNTABLE NOUN
A **terrace** is a flat area of stone or grass next to a building where people can sit.

tray COUNTABLE NOUN
A **tray** is a flat piece of wood, plastic, or metal that is used for carrying food or drinks.

treasure hunt COUNTABLE NOUN
A **treasure hunt** is a game in which players have to solve clues in order to win a prize.

trespass INTRANSITIVE VERB
If you **trespass** on someone's land, you go onto it without their permission.

trespasser COUNTABLE NOUN
A **trespasser** is someone who goes on someone else's land without their permission.

victim COUNTABLE NOUN
A **victim** is someone who has been hurt or killed by someone or something.

warm-hearted ADJECTIVE
A **warm-hearted** person is kind and friendly.

weapon COUNTABLE NOUN
A **weapon** is an object such as a gun or knife.

wicked ADJECTIVE
You use **wicked** to describe someone or something that is very bad in a way that will hurt people on purpose.

yacht COUNTABLE NOUN
A **yacht** is a large boat used for racing or for pleasure trips.

COLLINS ENGLISH READERS ONLINE

Go online to discover the following useful resources for teachers and students:

- Downloadable audio of the story

- Classroom activities, including a plot synopsis

- Student activities, suitable for class use or for self-studying learners

- A level checker to ensure you are reading at the correct level

- Information on the Collins COBUILD Grading Scheme

All this and more at **www.collinselt.com/readers**